The Past

AND

Future King

BOOK ONE OF THE
DAWN HERALD SERIES

WARREN M. MUELLER

BALBOA.
PRESS

A DIVISION OF HAY HOUSE

Balboa Press books may be ordered through booksellers or by contacting:

Balboa Press
A Division of Hay House
1663 Liberty Drive
Bloomington, IN 47403
www.balboapress.com
1 (877) 407-4847

Print information available on the last page.

ISBN: 978-1-5043-6981-7 (sc)
ISBN: 978-1-5043-6982-4 (hc)
ISBN: 978-1-5043-6980-0 (e)

Library of Congress Control Number: 2016919013

Balboa Press rev. date: 02/11/2017

Contents

PROLOGUE

IT WAS THE SECOND AGE of the earth, a time of peace and prosperity, where men ruled in scattered kingdoms interspersed with vast areas of wilderness. Most of what was known of the first age had passed into legend, then into fantasy, and was no longer considered relevant or worth remembering. Men were more concerned about accumulating wealth and enjoying the pleasures of life.

The Village of Downs End in the Kingdom of Glasford was one of a thousand such villages organized into a dozen kingdoms that spanned the earth. However, something unusual happened there one summer evening that had rarely happened during the earth's second age. An event that would transform lives and shake the foundations of life on earth.

The Village of Downs End was a quiet hamlet nestled in the rolling hills of the southern edge of the Kingdom of Glasford. There had been peace for a thousand years and people had settled into villages like Downs End. The people were mostly simple farm folk who did not travel much except to the village square for goods or to attend one of the many festivals they had throughout the year. There was a festival to celebrate the spring planting, the first crop, the second crop, and the first snow festival, as well as the longest and shortest days of the year festivals and so forth. Each of these festivals marked a break in the hard work and routine of village life and was eagerly anticipated. These festivals held many competitive events of various sorts to amuse and inspire the townsfolk. They were a self-sufficient people with strong traditions.

Success was generally measured in terms of land and livestock. Independence and self-sufficiency were highly valued and thus, farming was the most honorable profession. Those who did not farm were considered lower-class citizens because they were ultimately dependent upon the farmers. To travel beyond the village boundaries was considered risky business due to wolves and thieves. Occasionally, traveling merchants would bring the few goods that could not be produced locally.

The village was completely surrounded by a forest. There were three roads that ran to the north, south and west to other villages, which were generally one or more days' ride away by horseback. No roads ran to the east because the forest in that direction was considered enchanted and led to a snow-capped mountain range that could be seen in the distance.

It was common knowledge in Downs End that this forest was unnaturally old. Some said that the souls of departed relatives could sometimes be seen wandering in the enchanted forest when the moon was full. There were stories about hunters who ventured into the eastern woods never to be seen again. Even in the daylight farmers along the edge of this forest reported hearing strange sounds and seeing shadows moving among the ancient, crowded trees. A short distance into the enchanted forest was a lake fed by springs and streams that flowed from the mountains. This was as far as it was considered safe for anyone to venture into this forest.

DOWNS END

$\mathcal{I}$T WAS A WARM AND calm spring day when Bill Barley drove his wagon into the village of Downs End on the eve of the planting festival. The village was buzzing with last minute preparations. A young girl suddenly darted into the street in front of him chasing a cat that ran between the legs of the horse pulling his wagon.

"Whoa Shadow!" he shouted as he pulled hard on the reins.

Shadow showed his displeasure by raising up on his hind legs which caused the girl to fall backwards. Once he regained control, Bill said, "Best be watching where you chase that cat! You don't have as many lives to spare as him."

"Sorry sir", replied the girl as she quickly got up and continued her pursuit.

This commotion caught the attention of the village constable who was talking to a nearby group of peddlers. The constable was a jolly, rotund man who looked like a peasant except for his silver badge.

"Top o'the morning to you! I don't recall seeing you here before", said the constable as he approached the wagon.

"Right you are. This is my first visit to Downs End."

"Welcome! We are always glad to see more peddlers come to celebrate with us. Where are ye from?"

"The village of Ashford."

"Hmm, not familiar with that one. Must be a ways away."

"Aye, I have traveled south for two weeks to get here."

"Well, I know that our festivals are popular but this is the furthest I have ever heard of."

Bill looked down and fidgeted with the reins, before replying. "Actually, the festival is a fortuitous circumstance. My main business is the delivery of some special order books."

"Ahh! So you have come to see Willet our village scribe!"

"Yes, can you tell me where he lives?"

"I can do better than that if you give me a lift. He lives on the opposite side of the village."

Bill was unsure about this due to the size of the constable but he moved over as best he could. The entire wagon tilted to one side when he climbed aboard. The constable overlapped Bill's space so that he had to lean away.

"Thanks for the lift. Terrible hot day for this time of year, said the constable as he took out a handkerchief and dabbed his head.

"Now let me tell ye a bit about Willet as we go."

"Willet is a strange fellow even as scribes go. He rarely attends the festivals and keeps mostly to himself. He deals mainly in deeds, wills, and how-to types of books. Stays up well beyond a respectable bedtime reading books that he orders from strange places." He cast a sideways glance at Bill who forced a smile.

"Nobody knows where Willet came from, as he is the oldest living person in the village. He arrived years before even the eldest of the villagers could remember."

"That is odd," replied Bill as he wondered what Willet might look like.

"Some say he arrived with a rare company of knights. Others think that he was the orphan of a trader who was killed by wolves. There are even a few who say that he emerged from the enchanted forest."

"More than odd," Bill added.

The constable nodded in agreement.

"Although he is strange, we do appreciate his wisdom. He has read virtually every book in his shop and he likes to give advice. Mostly about farming and business. Rumor has it that sometimes he helps with improving the competitive skills of some of the winners of our festival events."

The constable gave Bill a wink and added, "I think this is just sour grapes as we run fair and honest competitions. However, most folks around here are not much for reading unless it had some practical value so Willet is consulted by many."

"Yonder is Willet's shop."

A young lad emerged from the entrance.

"Tom, I see you have another arm full of books, shouted the constable as they pulled up to the front.

"Yes sir, I can hardly wait to read these!" Tom replied as he passed by.

The constable whispered, "Strange lad. Almost as strange as Willet. Likes to read books and says he wants to be a scribe like Willet."

"Weird," Bill replied.

"Aye, especially since he is the only son of Throm who is one of the best farmers in the village. Some say his crops grow better because his farm adjoins the enchanted forest. Throm comes from a long line of farming families. I expect he will straighten his son out on this matter before too long. The course Tom is on is causing embarrassment to his parents. Not to mention the teasing he gets from other children who think he's strange."

The constable got out of the wagon and said, "pardon my rambling. I had best get about my business. Lot's to do before tomorrow."

CONFOUNDED FANTASY BOOKS

SEVERAL DAYS AFTER THE FESTIVAL, Tom went to Willet's shop to return some farming books for his father. He entered the shop, but the old man was not there.

"Willet! It's Tom. Are you here?"

This generally would rouse the old man as the adjoining room was his apartment. He called again but there was no response. Tom thought this was odd since Willet rarely left the shop except to buy food. Because Tom had delivered food to Willet the day before, he ruled out this possibility.

He noticed that the door to the adjacent room was open which was unusual. Tom approached the doorway to the apartment and looked inside. Like the shop, this room was filled with numerous books that were stacked on the floor and filled the shelves that covered the walls. There was a simple wooden bed and a few pieces of furniture, which were also covered with books.

Tom had never been in this room before and the sight of so many books surprised and delighted him. He entered cautiously so as to not disturb the piles of books, some of which reached almost to the ceiling. As he wandered about, he read some of the titles and noted that many of them had accumulated dust and appeared to be very old.

Near Willet's bed, he saw an old wooden trunk with strange carvings on it that appeared to be words in some unknown language. He went over to the trunk and ran his fingers over the carvings. The characters were smooth and eloquent but totally unlike anything he had ever seen. They were grouped like letters to form what Tom guessed must be words. As Tom was feeling the trunk, Willet suddenly appeared through a trap door in the floor.

"Must be getting old that I can't remember where I put my reading glasses…second pair that I have misplaced in the past month," he muttered to himself as he came up the stairs.

Willet was startled as he met Tom at the top of the stairs.

"Master Tom, what are you doing here?" Before he could answer, Willet said, "I see you have been drawn to my old trunk. Quite unusual, is it not? It was made long ago from a tree that no longer exists. However, even greater treasures lie within. Would you like to see?"

"Yes, please!" said Tom with eager anticipation.

The old man proceeded to pull a key from a leather necklace inside his shirt and went to open the trunk.

"I must warn you before I show you the contents. What you are about to see has the potential to radically change your life."

Tom replied, "I will gladly take the chance to learn more about these mysterious carvings. As you have said, my curiosity is aroused and I must know more about this."

"Very well, Master Tom. Look inside!"

Tom slowly lifted the lid and peered into the trunk. To his surprise, there was nothing inside but more books.

"You may be thinking that these are just more books, but they are much more than that."

Willet explained that these were books of history and legends of the first age of the earth.

"These books contain ancient knowledge that has passed from mankind."

"May I read them?" asked Tom.

"You may, but I must warn you that they will expand and transform your mind, for the words within them will come alive in you."

Tom eagerly grabbed several of them and, after thanking the old man, ran home to read them.

Over the next several weeks, Tom read the books. They contained stories of good and evil creatures like elves, werewolves, wizards, vampires, angels, and demons. These stories frightened and intrigued him so that the more he read, the harder it was to stop reading. The images inspired by the stories captivated his mind. He began to have dreams in which he became part of the stories.

There was one recurring dream that frightened him so much that he would wake up in a cold sweat. In this dream, he wandered to the nearby lake in the enchanted forest and drowned while swimming in the icy water.

Reality and his dreams seemed to merge. In his dreams, he relived an incident that happened to him at school in which he was teased and bullied by some boys. They pushed him down so that he fell backward and was looking up at them. As he lay on his back, they converged on him and taunted him. He could see their faces looking down at him.

Suddenly, their faces were transformed into hideous snarling beasts bending down to devour him, which jarred him out of his sleep.

Along with the nightmares, he also had wonderful dreams of flying over fantastic landscapes and kingdoms inhabited by elves. He dreamed of blessed places of peace and order in which there were angels and other beautiful creatures of good will. The pleasant stories and dreams made his village life seem small and insulated. He became restless to explore the possibility that the magical places he read about might exist in some far away land.

His parents took note of his increasingly incessant reading, which began to interfere with the completion of his farm chores. His mother wanted to ban him from reading books other than his schoolbooks, but his father felt otherwise.

"It's just a phase he's going through. Do you remember how I was when you met me? I too was captivated by the old man's books for a time, but I came to my senses and so will he. He's got too much farming in his blood to be anything else."

Nevertheless, his father kept an eye on Tom and, much to his dismay, noticed that he spent more and more time reading the fantasy books.

One day, Throm noticed that the chickens were running wildly to and fro as Tom absent-mindedly flung feed with one hand and read with the other.

His father approached him and said, "Tom, doing so much book reading is bound to confound your mind. Books are good if they teach you something practical, but they can cause unhappiness if they fill your mind with imaginary things that have no value."

He looked around and then urgently motioned for Tom to follow him into the barn saying, "Follow me. I want to show you something."

Throm led his son into the barn and proceeded to a feed bin which he opened. He reached inside and pulled up a loose board in one corner and took out a book wrapped in a rag.

"Here is an example of one of those useless and confounded fantasy books. I borrowed it from Willet many years ago and have kept it. I no longer read it because it put images in my mind of things that don't exist and that distracted me from being a successful farmer. Nevertheless, I could not bring myself to return it or destroy it for there is something haunting about it."

His father continued, "I never could quite understand the story and it gave me troubled dreams."

He paused and stared at the wrapped book and a look of sadness came over him as though he had lost or forgotten something. Then his mood changed and he seemed to gather himself and said, "Your mother was right when she advised me to keep my feet on the ground and not fill my head with nonsense that only leads to ridicule and ruin. I think it's best for you to return this book and the other fantasy books to Willet and stick to the practical sort."

Tom knew it was no good arguing, so he took the book from his father and the others and went to see Willet. As he walked to Willet's, he unwrapped the book his father gave him and looked at the title, *The Past and Future King*. Tom wondered why his father had kept this book hidden and so he was drawn to find out what it was about. He started to read it while he walked towards the scribe's shop, but he had only finished the first chapter when he arrived.

"Hello, Master Tom! Finished reading another batch of books?"

Tom's face told the old man that something was wrong.

"My father says I can not read any more fantasy books, but the stories are burned into my mind. I find myself thinking and dreaming about them more and more. There is one particular dream that troubles me where I jump into the lake by the enchanted forest to swim, but I drown. I have had this dream often and have even tried to change the ending but I cannot. It seems so real. What shall I do?"

The old man looked at Tom with compassion and said, "As a man thinks, so he becomes. I told you that these books were special and that they would transform your mind. A repeated dream that comes from reading these books is not to be ignored. Since your dream clearly revolves around the enchanted lake, you must go there to discover its meaning. When the moon is full, go to the lake and look at your reflection. As for reading more of these books, don't worry about that. A seed has been planted in you that will grow if you follow my advice."

ALTERED REALITY

*I*T WAS A CALM SUMMER evening when Tom quietly slipped out of his bedroom window and headed towards the lake. He could see surprisingly well in the silver moonlight of the full moon. He soon reached the enchanted woods and proceeded on a path to the lake that he had taken a few times before, but always in daylight.

The forest seemed alive with sounds and he took note of crickets, frogs, and owls. A few times he heard some unfamiliar bird calls and even a low growl but, even in the moonlight, he could not see far enough into the forest to identify the sources of the sounds. After hearing a much louder growl from the blackness of the woods nearby, fear gripped him, so he quickened his pace and arrived at a grass field adjacent to the lake.

He ran across the grass field and climbed onto a boulder next to the shore. Before him was an expanse of calm water that looked inky black except for the reflection of the moon and stars. Near the shore, the water was deep and clear. Tom could see the cobblestone bottom drop away into blackness close to the boulder. He began to think that this was a rather pleasant place when he heard the howl of a wolf somewhere in the enchanted forest. This shattered his pleasant thoughts and he remembered Willet's words to look at his reflection in the lake.

He gazed at his image in the lake for several minutes, but saw nothing unusual. He decided to return home when he noticed a small ripple on the glass-like surface of the lake that distorted his image. The ripple multiplied and then the surface of the lake began to swirl, forming a whirlpool. From the center of the vortex a voice called to him saying, "Take a leap of faith if you want to know the truth!"

Tom was petrified as he remembered his dream in which he drowned while trying to swim in this very lake. As he wavered, uncertain as to what to do, he heard more wolves howling and turned to see a pack emerge from the woods a short distance from the path. Their yellow eyes gleamed from their large shadow-like outlines. They crept slowly towards him, growling as they approached.

Tom briefly considered trying to run but decided his best chance was to jump into the lake and swim along the edge to a safer place near the shore. He turned and jumped from the boulder into the lake.

He felt a cold shock as he entered the icy water at the edge of the whirlpool. The water was much colder than anything he had ever felt before. He struggled to swim along the edge of the whirlpool but the vortex was pulling him away from shore. His arms and legs became heavy and he no longer felt the cold. Numbness overcame his ability to swim and he became sleepy. He soon lost consciousness and sank into the vortex.

Tom being drawn into whirlpool

"Wake up! We must hurry!"

Tom opened his eyes to find himself staring into the handsome face of a young lad with pointed ears! As he struggled to assess the situation, he noted that the moon was full and that he was on the shore of the lake near the place he had jumped in. However, he was completely dry and when he looked beyond the young lad he saw six large wolf-like creatures approaching on their hind legs. They had long claws on their forelegs, huge fangs, and yellow, piercing eyes.

"Werewolves! No time to lose!"

Quickly the lad drew a bow slung across his back and fired an arrow that pierced the eye of the nearest werewolf. With a screaming howl it dropped dead, while the others rushed forward with a collective snarl. Immediately, two more arrows found their mark and two more were slain with arrows in the heart and throat. As more arrows whistled overhead from somewhere in the night, the remaining creatures turned and dashed for the cover of the forest.

"This way! We must hurry!" yelled the stranger. "They will regroup and return in greater numbers! Follow me!"

Instinctively, Tom began to follow the strange lad up a narrow, rocky path between the enchanted forest and the lake. He noted with dismay that this direction was taking him away from his village and towards the mountains. He strained to keep up with the lad but he ran faster than anyone he had ever seen. The distance between them grew until he found himself chasing a silhouette in the moonlight. Snarling and growling sounds behind him told him that the werewolves were in pursuit and were gaining on him. As he rounded a turn in the trail, he had to jump to one side to avoid running into the strange lad, who had stopped in the middle of the trail.

"Quickly, hop onto my back! We must go faster!" he said. "They are approaching!"

Before Tom could say anything, the lad picked him up onto his back and they were moving faster than any human could run. He looked over the lad's shoulder and saw trees flying by on either side of the path. The wind in his face made him squint and he thought that this must be what it feels like for those who race horses at the festivals.

Soon Tom could hear rushing water and then saw a boulder-filled stream cascading into the enchanted lake. The lad did not slacken his pace once they reached the stream. They bounded from boulder to boulder like a frog leaping across a pond on lily pads until they reached the far shore.

Upon reaching the opposite side of the stream, Tom got off the lad's back and they turned to see numerous dark shapes crossing the stream on the boulders. The stranger drew his bow and fired an arrow, which joined a swarm of other arrows coming from the woods behind them. As the arrows reached their targets, Tom saw several shapes fall into the stream. A second round of arrows sent the remaining creatures retreating back into the woods on the far stream bank.

"Follow me!" the stranger ordered. "No time to explain! The night grows late and we don't have much time!"

They continued to run along a narrow path through the woods but this time Tom followed the lad. The lad did not run as quickly and seemed to adjust his pace to as fast as Tom could run. While they were running, Tom heard singing from afar that stopped suddenly and was replaced by many different voices singing all around them.

Tom asked, "What is that singing?"

The lad replied without turning or changing his pace, "The forest sentinels are signaling each other. They are saying that we are no longer being pursued."

Tom marveled, "I see nobody and yet some of the singing

seems close enough that it could come from right in front of me. How can this be? Are they ventriloquists?"""

The lad replied, "Your hasty assumption blinds you to the truth."

The lad sang a short melody and, when he finished, two forms dropped from the trees in front of and behind them and joined their running. They were clad head to knees in hooded cloaks that matched the colors of the surrounding forest. Their faces and legs were painted to match their cloaks, which explained their invisibility.

As they ran, Tom decided that he must be dreaming. He pinched himself and tried to wake up but to no avail. Finally, he decided to accept this strange experience with the hope that it would eventually make sense, or end abruptly when he stopped dreaming.

VALLEY OF GLAINNE

$\mathcal{A}$FTER RUNNING SEVERAL MILES FURTHER into the woods, Tom noticed that this forest was very old as the trees were larger than any he had ever seen. Although the trees were huge, they were not crowded together. They seemed to respect the space of each other such that moonbeams penetrated to the forest floor in a dappled pattern. Several times Tom thought he saw a tree quiver or bend as they passed but he quickly dismissed this as an illusion caused by the strange interaction of shadows and the patchy moonlight.

They entered a clearing and suddenly stopped. The moonlight was brighter here and Tom could see that his companions appeared to be of similar age and size as himself. Under their cloaks, they were dressed in buckskin with a short sword and they each carried a bow slung over their backs. Under their painted faces, Tom could see hints of fair skin. They, too, had pointed ears and similar facial features that suggested they were related.

The lad turned to Tom and said, "I apologize that the

circumstances of our meeting and subsequent need for urgency that have until now precluded a proper introduction. I am Cearl, son of Prince Caelin. Our companions are Eni and Osric, who were among those who assisted our escape from the werewolves."

At this introduction Eni and Osric both bowed and, wrapping their cloaks about them, disappeared into the night in the twinkling of an eye.

Cearl smiled and looked hopefully at Tom as he said, "I am your guardian and devoted companion. Perhaps you recognize me?"

At this, Tom realized that there was something familiar about the lad, but he could not figure out what it was.

"I have been with you many times in your dreams."

Cearl motioned for Tom to follow him, "Come, although the distance is now short, we must not delay."

"Where are we going?" Tom asked.

"To see my father, Prince Caelin, who will enlighten you to the limits of your ability to understand."

As Tom struggled to make sense of what was happening, Cearl led him a short distance to the top of a rocky ridge where he paused and motioned for Tom to take a look.

Cearl said, "This is the Valley of Glainne, the home of my people."

Below them was a broad valley surrounded by sheer mountain cliffs on three sides. Even in the moonlight, Tom was struck by the beauty of this valley, which reminded him of some of the pleasant magical places he had dreamed about. He had the feeling that he had been here before, but he had no clear recollection of it.

Everywhere within the valley was the sight and sound of

flowing water. There were three waterfalls on the far valley wall that plunged from the snow-capped heights of the mountains beyond. As they descended down a winding path to the valley floor, Tom saw numerous bubbling springs and cobblestone brooks that flowed into a lake in the center of the valley. There were lush forests of pine and fir interspersed with grass clearings bordered by huge fern groves. The fragrance of pine and balsam filled the air and he sensed that this was a blessed place of harmony and peace. The sky in the east was starting to lighten as they reached the valley floor.

Cearl said, "Look at the large lake and tell me, do you see any dwellings?"

"Just one small cottage near the side of the lake," Tom replied.

"It is enough, it is our destination," said Cearl. Taking Tom upon his back, he hurried down to the cottage.

As they approached the cottage, Tom could see that it was small and simple with a thatched roof and a single door and window. It looked quite inviting as a faint glow came from the window and an aroma of cooking food was carried by the smoke from the chimney. Tom got off of Cearl and they walked towards the door which suddenly burst open. A black figure stepped out and stood before them completely covered from head to foot in a hooded cloak. The figure's arms slowly raised in an embrace and then it moved towards them, Tom caught a glimpse of shining amour and the hilt of a large jeweled sword beneath the black cloak.

"Wes ou hal! Sir Egric! Long have I prayed for this meeting, however short it may be!"

"Sir, you must be mistaken." Tom replied, "I am Tom, son of Throm, a farmer in the village of Downs End."

"It is as you say. However, you are much more than you have said but you have yet to learn it."

"Please forgive me for confusing you. My name is Prince Caelin. I have waited many years hoping for this meeting. Your entry into this world marks your birth into a realm of greater awareness and possibilities. Relatively few of the race of men have experienced such a birth. Most do not have faith in what are popularly called legends and fantasy."

"A great feast was prepared by my people to celebrate your birth but the location of your entry and subsequent events have not made that possible. Nevertheless, I am grateful for even this humble meeting and that you have safely arrived. There are many things I must try to tell you in the short time remaining."

Prince Caelin continued, "Behold, the eastern sky brightens, the full moon wanes and dawn marks the end of our time together. Among those of your race who are born into this world, many perish soon after due to the evil one and his allies. The werewolves you met wanted to put an end to your life here shortly after your birth. It is fortunate that my son was familiar with your dreams and guessed correctly as to the place you would be found if you failed to appear here."

Tom asked, "How could I have found this place without Cearl's help?"

Prince Caelin explained that his was the voice Tom had heard from the center of the whirlpool.

"If you would have had enough faith to jump into the vortex, you would have emerged here and have avoided any perils. Your lack of faith and obedience could have been your ruin. It appears that the damage is limited to the short time I have to instruct you."

"Listen carefully and follow my instructions precisely or you could fall under the evil one's spell and think this is only a dream. This world is part of yours but it is separated by time and is what your world refers to as 'the first age of the earth.' The evil one has cast a spell upon mankind making them believe that all there is to life is the pursuit of pleasures and the accumulation of knowledge. This will be the first of many trials when you return to your world. You will be tempted to think that this is only a dream."

Prince Caelin placed his hands firmly on Tom's shoulders and looked deep into his eyes.

"If you accept this lie, it will result in the ruin of who you could become and many things that could otherwise be."

As Tom stared into the Prince's deep blue eyes, he sensed intense concern and hope. Their souls seemed to merge and Tom felt like he was falling into a vast blue ocean as his focus narrowed to the Prince's eyes.

A collage of images raced through his mind at tremendous speed. They seemed to be a glimpse of many things yet to come or perhaps of possibilities but Tom could not make sense of them as they passed in a brief blur.

The Prince relaxed his grip on Tom and continued, "The third age of the earth has not yet begun, but it will be the offspring of the merger of the first and second ages. Its beginning will mark the end of our worlds and it will be the ultimate fate of all things. I wish I could tell you more but our time is almost gone. However, there is one more thing that I must tell you before you go."

Withdrawing his hands from Tom's shoulders, the Prince

reached into his cloak and pulled out a smooth stone attached to a leather necklace.

"This is a seeing stone. It will help you to see beyond the physical appearance of people and things in your world, revealing their true nature. This stone will help you find your way. You must pass through many trials and despair but, if you have faith, you will prevail."

"You must learn how to use this stone after your return. You must seek out a mentor who will instruct you. When you return to your world, you will encounter a mighty warrior who will guide and protect you. To avoid falling under the evil one's spell, you must do exactly as he says once you awaken. Cearl will also be with you but you will not be able to see him or the stone until you learn to use it."

"It is time for your return!"

The Prince exclaimed, "Jump into the center of the vortex in the nearby lake before dawn or all is lost! Follow me!"

Prince Caelin ran towards a nearby alder thicket and disappeared, leaving Tom with Cearl. Before Tom could ask any questions, Cearl picked him up onto his back and ran to the edge of the lake where he put him down. He too disappeared in the twinkling of an eye saying, "Trust and obey."

Immediately, the water began to ripple and swirl. Once a vortex formed, Tom jumped into it. As before, he felt bone-piercing cold as the icy water enveloped him. His body was soon numb and he lost consciousness.

THE ENCHANTED LAKE

*I*T WAS DAWN WHEN TOM awoke in the spot where he had first looked into the lake. He was lying in tall grass next to a large boulder. He vaguely remembered jumping off the boulder into the lake. However, his clothes were dry, which was not possible if he had been in the lake.

"Perhaps I didn't fall into the lake but just fell asleep," he said to himself as he looked at his clothes. While he looked at himself, he remembered the seeing stone. When he looked down at his chest, there was no necklace. He began to think that the events from last night were just another one of his vivid dreams, when he suddenly heard the growls of a pack of wolves approaching from the nearby forest.

"This was one part that I wish was a dream," he mumbled as he stood up and looked about at his escape options.

Suddenly, he heard a shout and a small, wiry man clothed in animal skins jumped between him and the wolves.

"Take the path along the lake into the forest while I hold

off the wolves!" he yelled as he charged towards the wolves with nothing but a stout wooden staff.

Tom froze and quickly reviewed his options: he could jump into the lake again, take the path back to the village, fight the wolves, or take the suggested path into the enchanted forest. To fight seemed hopeless since there were a dozen wolves and he had no weapons. The lake seemed to lead to the same dream-like encounter with wolves from last night. The path to the village seemed the wisest and easiest choice.

"Move quickly!" the small bearded man shouted again as he brought the end of his staff down on the head of the lead wolf. "Take the path to the woods! I don't know how long I can hold them!"

The desperate urgency of his voice and selfless courage motivated Tom to obey and he instinctively began running towards the woods. The sounds of snarls and howls behind him told him that the little man was putting up quite a fight, but he did not dare to look back until he approached the tree line.

As he ran, his fear gave way to concern for the small stranger who bravely threw himself into harm's way to save him. A warm feeling seemed to grow from his chest and, as he looked down, he saw a faint glow. He turned around and looked back down the path to the edge of the lake and stared, dumbfounded, at the spectacle below. In the midst of the wolves he saw a large warrior in shining armor wielding a two handed broadsword. Beside him, Cearl was firing arrows at a frantic rate. There were a half dozen dead werewolves surrounding them and at least as many fleeing back into the woods. The warrior and Cearl turned and began to run up the path after him. The sight of the werewolves brought back nightmarish memories of the night before and spurred him to accelerate his pace on the path into the forest.

"I have no idea where I am going, but at least I won't be alone."

THE ENCHANTED FOREST

THE TREES SEEMED TO CLOSE in on the path as Tom ran deeper into the enchanted forest. He concentrated on putting as much distance as possible between himself and the wolves. When his legs felt heavy and his side ached, he stopped and listened for any sounds of pursuit. At first, he was relieved by the absence of any snarling and panting sounds. However, soon a different fear gripped him as he noticed that the forest was unnaturally quiet. There was not a bird, insect, or any other creatures stirring in these woods. The air was heavy with the smell of decaying leaves and branches, which made it seem like he was inside an ancient tomb. He continued to follow the path at a brisk walk and soon realized that the path took him ever deeper into the forest. The trees were getting larger and the canopy thicker.

"If this path continues to go deeper into these woods, it won't be long before there will be no light reaching the forest floor," he said to himself.

As he walked along the path, he began to think about the dangers he had been told about this forest.

"I wonder if ghosts really do wander this forest," he thought as he looked behind him. He started to worry as he thought about the stories he had been told of hunters who had ventured into these woods and never were seen again. He became frightened when he realized that he was already well beyond where even the bravest hunters must have dared to venture.

As his fears grew, he began to think about going back. "What happened to Cearl? Who was the little man or was he a tall warrior? Surely, they should have overtaken me by now, especially considering how fast Cearl could run."

"Perhaps I've taken a wrong turn on the path" he said to himself, but he could not remember any forks in the path.

"How foolish I am!" he thought as he reviewed his situation. "I'm alone in a forbidden forest, without food or water or having any idea where this path is leading me. By now my parents undoubtedly have discovered my disappearance and must be worried sick."

He imagined his parents frantically searching for him. He stopped and turned around retracing his steps back along the path. His mother's image came to mind and he could hear her saying, "Tom, keep your feet on the ground and stop dreaming about legends and fantasies. They will bring you confusion and keep you from being successful."

He thought, "I've been foolish to take this path. I should be going home."

He began to think that the adventures of last night were just a rather vivid dream when he suddenly stopped dead in his tracks and fear surged within him so that he stopped breathing. Before him was a wall of trees but no hint of the path! He tried to control a growing sense of panic by telling himself that he had gotten turned around while he was thinking and had reached the end of the path. Turning around he retraced his steps the way he had just come.

After a short distance, the path ended and he realized he was lost in the forest! He looked for any sort of landmark that could help him, but he saw nothing but an impenetrable wall of trees in every direction. Alone and lost in the enchanted forest, despair overwhelmed him and he sat down and cried.

In the midst of his grief he looked down and the image of the seeing stone came to his mind.

He remembered the faint glow and warm feeling on his chest when he chose this path. Then he recalled Prince Caelin's words: "Through trials and despair you will find your way."

These words stirred a faint sense of hope that the seeing stone could help him. Immediately, his mind countered that it was illogical to believe in an invisible stone given to him in a dream! Conflicting thoughts and emotions swirled in his head until he finally shouted, "Enough! I must decide whether my dream is real or dismiss it."

He decided that to continue to remain in this confused and uncertain condition would drive him insane. He thought of the brave little man who risked his life to save him from the wolves.

"Who was he and why would he do such a thing?"

Tom was sure that he had followed him into the woods. Tom remembered that the little man had told him to take this path into the forest. This gave Tom hope that the little man knew these woods and would find him.

As he wondered about these things, Tom felt a small weight on his chest. He looked down and saw a faint glow coming from where he sensed the stone should be. As he looked down at his feet at the source of the mysterious glow, the path reappeared beneath his feet!

A surge of relief and hope welled up within him causing the glow to intensify, which further illuminated the path! Soon he found his way back to the place on the path where he had stopped and turned back. He began to realize that though he was alone, there was some power at work that was helping him. He felt connected to others of good will through the stone. This gave him a sense that he was fulfilling some important, yet undefined, purpose. He felt excited and scared because he could no longer deny that he had begun a journey of great personal importance. He sensed that this journey had already changed him so that he could not return to the lad he once was.

When Tom faced the direction that led deeper into the forest, the path was visible. When he turned to return the way he had come, there was only darkness.

"Seems like I have no choice," he said to himself as he shrugged and followed the light.

He continued on the path in the glow of the invisible stone. The forest canopy became so thick that light no longer penetrated to the forest floor. The uncanny silence continued except for an occasional rustle of leaves in the underbrush but he did not see anything. The path appeared to be gradually sloping downward and the land surrounding the path was getting rocky. He was hungry, thirsty, and felt like he had not slept in days.

"I must at least find water and a place to rest soon," he mumbled to himself.

He thought about calling for the little man but he realized that he did not know what to call him. After walking for several more hours, shadows started to play tricks with his mind. He had the uneasy feeling that he was being watched. Several times he thought he caught a glimpse of someone or something quickly moving from boulder to boulder parallel to his path.

Once or twice he stopped suddenly and thought he heard a brief rustling of leaves as though he was being tracked. He started to think of arming himself with a wooden staff, if he could find a suitable branch along the path. As his fear grew, the light from the stone diminished and the shadows grew closer.

"Wes ou hal! Sir Egric! At last I have found you!"

Out of the shadows stepped the little man that had saved him from the wolves at the lake. "I lost the path but was able to find you by the glow of the stone."

"Who are you and why do you call me Sir Egric?"

The little man bowed and replied, "I am called Wini, a shepherd of the plains of Redwald. I have raised many sheep and have faced wolves, bears, and lions to keep them safe. I have suffered numerous wounds but have never lost even one lamb entrusted to my care."

As Wini talked, Tom could sense his great passion and dedication for his sheep.

"I do miss them terribly! I pray for their safety and take comfort in the fact that my kinsmen will watch over them. As for the second part of your question, I call you Sir Egric because that is the name Prince Caelin called you."

"Prince Caelin! Then you have seen him too! I could not have been dreaming unless it is possible for two strangers to share the same dream! Tell me, what did he look like?"

Wini described him just as Tom had seen him.

Tom asked, "Did he say anything to you?"

Wini said the Prince told him that he had entered a realm that was considered part of the past by his people but still existed along side of his world.

"He said that I must protect you as I had my sheep. He said that you would guide me to a seer who would teach me many things and help me understand my destiny. He described the place I would find you and the path we were to take. Then he told me to jump into the nearby lake when I saw the vortex form. However, he didn't tell me of the danger I would face when I found you, which has delayed our formal meeting until now."

Tom felt a strange mixture of relief and despair as Wini described his meeting with the Prince. He was now convinced that they had both experienced an expanded reality and state of being. However, he became frightened by the revelation that Wini did not know his way through the forest and that he was trusting Tom to lead him!

"My name is Tom, son of Throm, the farmer. I prefer that you call me by the name I am accustomed to."

"As you wish, Master Tom," replied Wini.

Although a grown man, Wini was about the same height and build as Tom. He had dark skin and short black hair and a beard. Tom guessed he must be twenty years older than himself. Tom noticed Wini had a leather pouch at his side hanging from a strap over one shoulder.

"Do you have anything to eat or drink?" he asked.

Wini nodded and reached into the pouch producing a large, dried mushroom cap.

"Prince Caelin gave me this pouch. He said it had food for our journey. It only contains a few mushroom caps and some strange berries that I have never seen before."

Tom had not eaten since the previous day and he eagerly ate half the mushroom cap and a hand full of berries. The mushroom cap was delicious and seemed to swell in his stomach so that it gave him a full feeling. The berries were tart but juicy and satisfied his thirst so that he was quite content. Wini likewise quickly devoured some food and they soon resumed their journey through the forest.

Tom judged it to be mid-afternoon but it seemed like dusk since the thick forest canopy and dense undergrowth filtered out most of the daylight. The light from the stone continued to illuminate the path, which made it seem like they were blazing a trail that could not be duplicated. Although Tom still felt uneasy about where they were going, he decided to trust the light from the stone and followed the path.

Wini seemed content to follow Tom.

"I'm glad I have you to guide me," he said. "These woods are not like the plains of my homeland. There I could always find my way by the stars."

After a short while, Wini looked around and again expressed his confidence in Tom and his gratitude to be following him.

At first, Tom felt guilty and almost told Wini that his confidence was misplaced. However, he thought that telling Wini would only instill fear, which he was trying to manage within himself. Wini's cheerful spirit and confidence in Tom gave him hope. Tom sensed that he was fulfilling a role that he had been empowered to perform. He remembered Cearl's last words to him before he returned to this world, "Trust and obey."

The path continued to gradually descend and, after several hours of walking, they entered a ravine. The forest trees were not as old and the canopy less dense. Tom could see from the angle of the sunbeams high up on the eastern wall of the ravine that it would soon be dark. He was beginning to think about finding shelter for the night when he heard the sound of water just ahead. This sound reminded him of how thirsty he was.

They both looked at each other and, without another word, ran towards the sound. After a short distance, they came to a small waterfall spilling into a pool of water. Although they were both thirsty, they stopped near the edge of the pool and stared up at the waterfall. Water plunged from a cave in the rock about halfway up the ravine wall. The water fell a hundred feet into a crystal clear pool. Tom noticed a rainbow in the mist that rose from where the water hit the pool. As he admired the beauty before him, he suddenly realized that the waterfall was at the end of the ravine!

Tom was shaken and instinctively looked down at his chest. "The stone still glows," he said to himself.

As he struggled with his fears and uncertainty as to what to say or do, Wini exclaimed "Forgive me, Master Tom for I must confess I was starting to be concerned about where we would spend the night. This is not only a great place to sleep but there is clean water as well!"

Tom was about to explain that he knew nothing of this place, but Wini had already run to the edge of the pool and jumped in. Tom noticed that there was a shallow indentation in the rock face near the waterfall and plenty of loose leaves for bedding.

"At least we have reasonable shelter for the night," he muttered to himself as he followed Wini into the water.

After bathing and eating the rest of the mushrooms and berries, they settled down on a thick bed of leaves that they placed inside the depression in the rock face.

It was a calm, starry night much like the previous one. Wini continued to thank Tom for his guidance and his company. He seemed quite content in his faith in Tom and in what Prince Caelin had told him. Soon Wini was sound asleep while Tom continued to stare at the stars wondering what he should do when morning came.

As he laid on his back, deep in thought, he suddenly had the sense that something was wrong. He sat up and looked around. Everything seemed normal except that it was very quiet. Then he noticed that the waterfall had stopped flowing and the pool reflected the moon and stars like a mirror.

"What an odd and beautiful sight," he thought as he moved to the edge of the pond to take a closer look. As he crouched down and bent over the water, the mirror-like surface of the pool transformed into a window through which Tom saw a large table filled with food!

There was roast turkey, sweet potatoes, fresh loaves of bread, fruits and vegetables of various sorts. A pig on a spit was roasting over a stone hearth. There were also pastries and plum pudding on a smaller table near the hearth.

Tom suddenly felt very hungry. He was mesmerized by the inviting image and he reached out to touch the surface of the water. His hand seemed to be drawn into the image and he felt like he was falling through a window into the room.

As he passed through the surface of the pool, he heard Wini shout, "No! Master Tom!"

He felt pressure on his legs pulling him back out of the water.

ANDHUN

$\mathcal{T}$OM AND WINI FELT THEMSELVES falling. In the blink of an eye, they found themselves on their hands and knees looking up at a long wooden table filled with food. The aromas of fresh baked bread and roasted meat filled the room.

"I'm so hungry I could eat till Tuesday!" exclaimed Tom. He quickly sat down and eagerly began eating whatever was within his reach.

"Master Tom, please don't ever go anywhere without me. I almost got separated from you!"

As Tom proceeded to stuff his mouth with a turkey leg, Wini looked around and said, "Strange that no one is around. This certainly looks like a nice place. I hope that whoever lives here doesn't mind our bad manners."

As Tom continued to eat he wondered if this was the home of the mentor that would guide them. Tom thought, "Surely this food and pleasant surroundings must be the reason why Prince Caelin only gave us a small amount of food for our journey. Also, the light from the stone had led them to this place. How foolish he was to have doubted the guiding light of the stone! Even though the path appeared to end in a blind canyon there was a hidden portal to this place. But, where was this place?"

"Welcome, young ones! I am glad you have arrived!"

A kind-looking old man dressed in a long white robe emerged from the doorway beyond the head of the table.

He smiled at them and said, "Help yourselves to whatever you want. My name is Andhun. I am the keeper of this place."

Andhun asked, "Who are you?"

"My name is Tom, son of Throm, and this is Wini. Please tell us about this place. I sense we have returned to Prince Caelin's world."

Andhun replied, "It is as you have said. I am an old friend of Prince Caelin. You must be a special friend of his for I see he has given you a seeing stone, which is a very rare and precious gift."

Andhun paused and seemed to drift away in his thoughts for a moment as he gazed at the stone. Then he said, "Forgive me for interrupting your dinner. Come, let us eat and you can tell me the events that led you here."

Tom and Wini both remarked at the excellent selection and abundance of food. They sat down and ate voraciously. They took turns telling small parts of the strange events that led them to this place.

Andhun listened intently while Tom spoke about the previous day. He thought for a moment and then said, "Have no fear, for you are safe here. I will instruct you both on the paths that lie before you."

Andhun was a very generous and attentive host. He

insisted that they try most of what was on the table until Tom and Wini were quite full. Andhun was tall and thin with grey eyes and a long white beard that matched the length of his hair. Tom noted a long wooden staff covered with strange symbols and a pointed hat on a peg on the wall near the fireplace. He also had a silver chain around his neck from which hung a medallion that had an intricate design that Tom could not make out. After the turbulent events of the previous day, Tom felt relieved and content to be in comfortable surroundings with a pleasant host.

"Andhun, please tell us about this place," Tom asked.

"Very well," Andhun replied. "I see you are anxious to begin your education. There is much to learn. Let's begin with a tour of the accommodations."

"Follow me."

Andhun rose from the table, picked up his staff and hat and headed through the doorway. He led them through a long hallway with many doors on either side. The hallway was carpeted and decorated with paintings of wealthy and noble looking people. Tom noticed that they had the same medallion around their necks that Andhun carried.

Andhun said, "This place is a center of learning and I am the head master. The paintings are some of our former students who have achieved positions of power and wealth. These doors lead to the rooms of some of our students. It is late and most of our students have retired for the evening."

The hallway brought them to a large hall with several fireplaces. There were statues and groups of ornate tables and comfortable chairs. A fountain and a small pond were in an octagonal depression in the center of the hall. There were tapestries and paintings of various sorts on the walls. The polished wooden floor was tastefully covered with a variety of colorful rugs.

Andhun said, "Come, I will show you the library and then to your room."

Andhun led them past the fountain in the center of the hall to two large wooden doors. Tom noticed that these doors had rows of wooden panels that were engraved with various animals and human figures. He was about to ask about them when Andhun pushed them open. Tom and Wini stopped in the doorway and stared in awe into the library, which was as big as the great hall. Tom had never seen so many books in one place. There were floor to ceiling bookcases everywhere and rolling ladders that were at least twenty feet tall.

Andhun seemed amused by the dumbfounded look on their faces and said, "This is the largest collection of books in the old earth. There is one book that is the foundation upon which all other knowledge is based."

Andhun led them to a circular pedestal upon which a large and very ancient book was opened.

He showed them the cover which contained some strange letters that were reminiscent of those on Willet's trunk.

"What do these characters say?" Wini asked.

Andhun replied, "It is an ancient tongue. The title of the book is, *The Once and Forever Ruler.*"

"This book is unique in that it is to be experienced rather than read. It shows each person the truths in life they need to understand their destiny."

Andhun opened the book and said, "Let's begin your training. I must warn you that the words of this book will change to images that will reveal deep truths to each of you at a personalized level. Your readings of this book may show you things about yourself that you do not realize. Your readings will also reveal the future and impart knowledge that will empower and enlighten you."

Andhun continued, "Because the words of this book are so powerful, your first reading will be limited. Your exposure will increase gradually as your mind expands and your training progresses.

I must caution you not to gaze too long into this book as what you experience could overwhelm your mind and result in insanity. Therefore, I will join you in this reading, which will be limited to the introductory pages."

Andhun began to read and then chant the words on the first page. As he did so, the words gradually faded and images appeared. Andhun continued by narrating the images.

"In the first age of the earth, the Creator of all things resided with a great host of creatures in the vast expanse of the universe. There was perfect love, peace, and harmony expressed in fantastic musical symphonies beyond description or comprehension. These symphonies were ever changing, yet unified in their adoration for the Creator.

In the midst of one of these symphonies, something without precedent happened. One of the angels decided to draw attention to himself by playing discordant sounds. Other angels joined in and contributed to the unpredictable and clashing sounds. There arose a dispute among the angels so that they no longer were unified and harmonious. The discordant music had a strange power that made it stand out from all the other blended sounds.

The angels that played this music claimed to have discovered a new type of knowledge. By disrupting the heavenly symphonies with their music, they became the center of attention. Their self-assertion and independence filled them with pride. They refused to blend or harmonize with the other creatures and started creating music as though none but themselves existed. These angels became known as the Demonians.

The Creator decided to remove and contain this rebellion by banishing the Demonians to the earth. He chose one of their leaders called Devlin and made him ruler over the earth and all its creatures. He gave Devlin the task of reunifying the angels. In order to deal with their pride, the Creator required the Demonians to serve mankind. They were to protect, guide, and instruct mankind, but they had to remain invisible so they would not receive any acclaim, which could add to their pride. If Devlin could reunify the angels and bring harmony to mankind, the Creator promised to restore their place in heaven and he would become the once and forever ruler of the earth. Unfortunately, some of the Demonians rebelled against Devlin and took physical forms, intermarrying with the daughters of men. Their union with mankind produced distorted offspring such as vampires, orcs, trolls, werewolves, and monsters of various sorts that were collectively called Titans.

The Titans preyed upon mankind and threatened to destroy them but Devlin pleaded for them and for help from the Creator. The Creator responded by removing the remnant of mankind from the first age of the earth. He created another earth separated from the first one by a time barrier. The two earth ages were connected by portals that allowed Devlin to work towards reuniting all the creatures. The Creator saw that Devlin needed more help to restore peace and directed the obedient angels known as the Aigneis to assist him. The Aigneis took material form and became the ancestors of the elves. When unity among the creatures of both earths is achieved, the Creator will consolidate both earth ages into a third age of peace, prosperity, and harmony. This is the goal of Devlin and all those who follow him."

The images faded and words reappeared on the pages as Andhun closed the book.

"In future readings you will learn more of the brotherhood of Devlin and take your places in prominent positions arranged for you in your world. Come, it is time to show you to your room."

Tom asked, "If monsters roam this world, how is this place not destroyed?"

Andhun smiled and said, "Through our learning, we have achieved a level of knowledge and magic that protects us from the Titans. We are the vanguard of the human race, reclaiming mankind's rightful place in the first age of the earth!"

A short distance down another hallway from the library, Andhun stopped and opened a door to a bedroom chamber. Tom was impressed with the inviting and sophisticated appearance of the room.

"I hope you find everything to your liking. If not, please tell me in the morning and adjustments will be made."

As Andhun turned and started to exit the room he said, "There is one important rule that I must insist that you follow for your safety. When the gong sounds, you must remain in this room until morning."

Andhun smiled and said, "I am glad that you have joined us and I look forward to seeing you grow in knowledge, wisdom and power. Good evening and pleasant dreams to you both."

After Andhun left, Tom exclaimed, "Isn't this the most wonderful place! Look, we each have a canopy bed with silk sheets!"

Wini frowned and said, "Beds are too soft for those such as I who are accustomed to sleeping on the ground. I would prefer to sleep on the floor. Even though this place is nice, there is something that just doesn't seem right. It's like when there's a lion prowling in the underbrush but I can't tell exactly where it's hidden."

"Nonsense, Wini! Andhun is a wonderful mentor and I believe there is much that he will teach us."

Wini replied, "Andhun troubles me. I could have sworn that Prince Caelin said that the mentor we seek was known to you."

"Wini, your nerves are just frazzled from the strange events of the day and you are overtired. Let's get some sleep," Tom said as he threw himself onto a bed.

"Ahh! Perfumed sheets as well! What a treat!"

Tom quickly fell asleep while Wini stretched out on the floor and stared at the ceiling. It wasn't long before Wini heard a gong and, despite his misgivings, he fell into a deep sleep.

Wini awoke in a cold sweat and crept over to Tom's bed. He placed one hand over Tom's mouth and shook him with the other.

"Master Tom, wake up! We must flee this place!"

Tom opened his eyes and started to mumble something but Wini said, "I just received a warning in a dream that we must return to the portal immediately. The message was from an elf lad called Cearl. He said we were in grave danger!"

Wini's urgent voice, intent gaze and pale face jolted Tom from a peaceful sleep. He briefly thought that Wini must have had a nightmare until he considered that Wini had mentioned Cearl's name. Since Tom had never mentioned Cearl's name, he realized the message must be real.

Wini led Tom down the deserted hallway and into the library. Although there were no lamps or torches burning, the night was ending and dawn's first light was beginning to dispel the darkness. Light beams from the waning full moon penetrated the ceiling of the library through a skylight and rested on the podium where *The Once and Forever Ruler* was displayed.

Tom was captivated by the enchanted appearance of *The Once and Forever Ruler,* which seemed to glow faintly in the moonlight. Wini dispelled the moment by saying, "Something is following us. We must hurry!"

They ran through the library and into the great hall where Wini stopped to grab a pike from a full suit of armor.

Tom whispered, "I don't see or hear anything. I think the shadows are playing tricks with your imagination."

"Shh!" whispered Wini, "Look there!"

Wini pointed to the doorway to the library. Tom saw nothing until suddenly a large shadow appeared and approached them silently on four legs. As it drew near, Tom saw that it was a large, hairy animal with long fangs and yellow eyes.

"Saber tooth tiger!" Wini whispered, "Run!"

They both turned and dashed down the hallway with the portraits and many rooms that led to the banquet room.

Wini soon realized that the saber tooth tiger was much too quick and would overtake them before they got to the banquet room. He could hear the beast's growls getting closer and closer. When he sensed that the animal was almost upon them, he grabbed the nearest door handle, flung open the door, and braced himself against it. The tiger bounded into the door with a crash that momentarily knocked it senseless. Tom was amazed that such a small man could withstand an impact that knocked the door off its hinges. While the tiger remained dazed on the floor, they ran and reached the doorway to the banquet room.

The room appeared as before except the food was gone and, at the far end of the table, there was a circular window through which they could see the last remaining stars. Suddenly, a familiar voice called to them from the window.

"Jump through the window when you see my image! You must act quickly! I don't know how long I can hold the portal open!"

They took a few steps towards the portal and then stopped dead in their tracks. They stared with horror as another large shadow with yellow eyes emerged from beneath the far end of the table.

Wini shouted, "Another tiger! Get onto the table!"

Wini lowered his pike as the tiger crept slowly out from under the table snarling and hissing. It stared intently at them as it crouched ready to spring upon them. As they faced this menace, Tom could hear shouting and sounds of confusion coming from the hallway that they had just left. Turning towards this noise, Tom froze as the shadow of the first cat appeared in the doorway. They were trapped!

The voice from the window began to chant words in a

strange tongue. The image of the night sky slowly faded and that of Willet appeared!

Wini shouted, "Put you arms around my neck and hold on!"

As Tom did so, Wini ran to the edge of the table and planted the pike onto the floor. They vaulted over the crouching beast and through the window with Tom clutching his neck before either of the tigers could react and catch them.

The Truth Be Told

Tom and Wini passed through the portal and emerged beside the pond where they had fallen in. Willet grabbed Tom and gave him a hug that lifted him off of his feet.

"I cannot tell you how happy I am to see you again, Master Tom! First I thought you had been killed, and then I was worried you were lost in the forest. My greatest fear was realized when I learned that you had been trapped by Andhun. It is remarkable that we are together again!"

Tom was astonished to see Willet and clung tightly to his neck weeping for joy.

"Willet, dear friend! How did you find me?"

"I am the mentor that Prince Caelin told you about and this is the place we were to meet at. I was waiting here for you and became anxious about the delay in your arrival."

"I was lost in the enchanted forest," replied Tom.

"Yes, I know. Cearl told me," responded Willet.

"He said your doubts had caused you to lose the path. When I heard this, I left this place to find you. Apparently, you recovered your faith in the seeing stone and must have arrived while I was searching for you."

Willet put Tom down and asked, "Who is your companion?"

"Tom put his arm around Wini and said, "This is Wini, my most excellent companion and faithful friend!"

Willet bowed and said, "I am Willet, the one promised by Prince Caelin to instruct you!"

Wini returned the bow and said, "I am most honored and relieved to meet you Master Willet!"

Willet turned and motioned for them to follow him, "Come, I will take you to a safe place where we can discuss your adventures."

Willet led them to a depression in the rock face where he had intended them to spend the night. It was sunrise and the first beams of sunlight were hitting the top of the ravine above the waterfall. Willet walked directly up to a sheer rock face between the waterfall and the depression in the rock face and, raising both arms, chanted some strange words. Immediately, the light beams at the top of the ravine traveled down the sheer rock face and illuminated a stairway in the rock that had been invisible. Tom and Wini stared in amazement as the light beams spread down each step of the stairway until the last one at their feet became apparent.

With a sheepish grin Willet said, "I apologize for the dramatics, but it is necessary to keep this place hidden."

As they ascended the staircase Tom looked down at the pool below the waterfall and noticed that the water was bubbling and steaming. Willet followed Tom's gaze and said, "That portal is unstable and is now closed. Andhun cannot pass but he shows his displeasure at your escape. Watch your step. We are nearly there."

Tom became unnerved when he looked back at the steps and noticed that they disappeared once they had passed over them. Looking ahead, Tom saw that the waterfall spilled from a cave about half way up the ravine wall. They soon arrived at the mouth of the cave and proceeded on a path to its rear, where the water flowed out of the rock under a large boulder.

Willet walked up to the boulder and put his face close to it. He then whispered some words that Tom could not understand and the boulder changed shape. A door appeared and slowly swung open revealing a large room lit by a shaft of light from a hole in the ceiling. There was water falling along the far wall of the room that flowed across it to the entrance in a shallow groove on the floor. The room was otherwise empty except for a few rocks fashioned like chairs and a large water basin shaped like a giant clamshell.

"Sit down and make yourselves comfortable!"

Willet sat down on a rock next to the basin and motioned for them to do the same.

Tom asked, "Is this your home?"

Willet laughed and said, "I have been accused of being strange but never of living like a cloistered monk. Don't worry. I am accustomed to more comfortable accommodations. This is but an entrance room to my home."

Pointing to the clamshell basin, Willet said, "This is the portal through which we will pass at dusk. There are many portals. Some, like this one, are stable and lead to predictable locations. Others, such as the one you passed through, appear and disappear without pattern; their destinations are ever changing. However, most portals only work at night. For now, let's pass the day recounting your adventures."

Tom and Wini described the events that led to their encounters with Prince Caelin and Andhun. Willet scowled when Tom mentioned their reading of *The Once and Forever Ruler.*

"That book is a clever perversion of the sacred book *The Past and Future King.*"

Willet continued, "Andhun was once a pupil of mine in training to be a member of the Order of Alastrine. This Order is composed of mentors, prophets, and magicians dedicated to the awakening of mankind."

Willet paused for a moment and a heavy sadness came over his face.

"Andhun was an exceptional pupil, bright and quick to learn. He so impressed the elves that some thought he was the first of those who would fulfill the prophecies of the dawning of the final age of the earth. He even had the very seeing stone that you possess around your neck."

"Unfortunately, his exceptional abilities made him very proud and impatient to hasten the dawning of the final age. This caused his downfall as he came under the influence of the Demonians."

"Fallen angels?" Tom asked.

"Yes", Willet replied.

"The Demonians gave Andhun knowledge and enhanced his memory so that he became one of the most learned and powerful to have ever lived among men and elves. He began to have visions of the third earth age in which he saw himself with Devlin reigning in a perfect world of peace and harmony. In this third earth age, there was no sickness, want or death.

He became obsessed with making his visions a reality. It was soon afterward, that he claimed to have received a revelation from an angel of light directing him to write a book called *The Once and Forever Ruler*.

Andhun proclaimed that his book represented a more accurate and detailed explanation of *The Past and Future King*. He was so persuasive in speech, wisdom, and magical powers that all but a few of those born into the first age of the earth followed him. They established a great center of learning from which they sent out influential graduates who attained high positions in the second age of the earth. These graduates are many of the prominent leaders and influential people who have brought peace and prosperity to the second age of the earth. They have formed a brotherhood of good intentioned people loyal to each other and their cause. Andhun and his followers are convinced that they have found a better path that will hasten the third age of the earth. In fact, they are unwitting pawns in the service of the Demonians, who manipulate them through deception."

Willet's shoulders sagged as if he was under a heavy burden of guilt. He looked very old and tired as he continued.

"Because of the success of Andhun, most men are content to pursue pleasures and few are interested in what is popularly considered fantasies. Thus, for the past one thousand years, few have been born into the first age and those who have been were either killed soon after their birth by evil creatures or have joined the cause of Andhun."

"Except for us," said Wini.

With a weary smile Willet replied, "Quite true. I am thankful for your escape."

"Tell us of Devlin," asked Tom.

"Is he good or evil?"

Willet replied, "The answer to that question will be evident from the truthful telling of the story you heard from Andhun. Much of what you were told is true, but therein lies the strength of the deception. By wrapping truth around lies, it makes them believable."

Willet continued, "What you were told was true except that Devlin led the Demonians in an attempt to get other creatures to join in their discordant music. Devlin and the other Demonians have been banished to the earth where they seek to create a kingdom that will enslave all its creatures to his will. During the first age of the earth, Devlin attempted to accomplish this by force. He commanded the Demonians to intermarry with men. This produced an army of new and monstrous creatures. These included vampires, orcs, and werewolves and have been collectively called the Titans. The Titans consider Devlin their Master. In fact, they worship Devlin since they have never known the true Creator and have been told lies since their birth."

"To prevent mankind from being destroyed, the Creator removed them from the first age and established a second earth age separated from the first, yet connected through time portals. He charged the remaining angels, or Aigneis, with the task of defending mankind and helping them establish a third earth age that would counter the evil purposes of Devlin. The elves are the physical manifestation of the Aigneis on the earth."

"*The Past and Future King* is the principal book of many that you will study at my home. The books you will study there contain the collective wisdom and experience of the elves, who seek the merger of the first and second earth ages into a third one that honors and glorifies the Creator."

Wini asked, "How will this happen?"

Willet smiled and replied, "Patience, Master Wini. You ask a simple question to a complicated series of events. There is much you will learn that will provide insights to your question. There also remains much to be revealed."

Willet paused and considered how much more to say.

"There is a prophecy that says the sons of light will herald the dawn of the third age."

"Who are the sons of light?" asked Tom.

Willet replied, "They are those of the race of mankind who have been born into the first age and are chosen by the Creator to be nobles in the third age. The prophecy says that these nobles shall prepare the way for The Past and Future King to rule over the final age of the earth."

Wini suddenly smiled as he recalled what Prince Caelin had called Tom and shouted, "Sir Egric! Master Tom, Prince Caelin called you Sir Egric!"

Tom blushed and became embarrassed and confused.

Willet said, "It is true that Prince Caelin thinks you are the first of the sons of light and I respect his opinion. However, this was also the opinion of some elves regarding Andhun."

Wini's brow became furrowed as he struggled with trying to understand what Willet had said.

Willet looked at his troubled expression and said, "Master Wini, is something bothering you?"

Wini replied, "If the Order of Andhun has produced peace among mankind for a thousand years and he was your pupil, you would be over a thousand years old!"

Willet replied, "Quite true, I am one thousand three hundred and eleven years old."

Willet laughed at the look of astonishment on the faces of Tom and Wini and said, "The Creator has blessed some prophets and learned men with knowledge to extend life. The aging process can be slowed with the proper training. It is something that you may also learn in time."

TALIESIN

$\mathcal{W}$ILLET, TOM AND WINI SAT in silence while they watched the shaft of sunlight entering the roof of the cave slowly fade. Tom wondered how such an ordinary looking person as Willet could be so old.

Willet stretched and said, "The day grows late and soon it will be time to depart for my home. Before we leave this place, I want to tell you about myself."

Willet leaned back in his chair and gazed up in the air. He seemed to go into a trance as if reaching back into the recesses of his mind that he had not used for many years. His golden brown eyes seemed to focus somewhere far beyond the roof of the cave. The lines on his forehead deepened as he concentrated and he absent mindedly stroked his grey beard.

"I did not know my parents for I was a baby when I was adopted by a childless merchant couple who wandered among the villages buying and selling whatever they could. My adopted parents said they never met my father. My mother was very poor and sold me to a better life.

I had a birth mark on my forehead that some people thought was bad luck, so my adopted parents hid it by making me wear a stocking hat. The elves believed differently and that my birth mark was a sign of blessing. There was a prophecy that a great teacher with a mark that fit the size and shape of mine would mentor the Sons of Light. As a result, an elf princess called Linette took a personal interest in me.

I enjoyed the vagabond lifestyle of my adopted parents. They taught me many practical lessons about interacting with people. They said that things were to be used but not desired as they all eventually became worthless.

"Things are not always what they seem," my father would say.

"One man's junk is another man's treasure."

He used to tell me to observe people closely. He would say, "The asking price is proportional to the desire of the buyer."

They taught me to look beyond appearances in order to judge both men and things correctly. They were loving and simple folks who had nothing more than a covered wagon full of goods and an old mule called Poky.

My step parents carefully planned their trips so that they always traveled during daylight. In this way, they would arrive at an inn or town well before sunset and avoid bandits and wolves. However, one day, when I was still a young lad, we got a late start and found ourselves in the enchanted forest at dusk. My father was walking next to Poky and my mother was sitting in the driver's seat of the wagon while I was sleeping in the back.

Suddenly, a large wolf appeared in the road not twenty paces in front of Poky which caused him to rear and panic.

Before my father could settle him, he bolted which caused my mother to fall out of the wagon. Poky turned and ran back down the road we had just traveled. I was shaken from my sleep and, as I looked out the back of the wagon, I could see many wolves converging on my parents while others were running after the wagon. It was the last I saw of my parents.

Poky ran as fast as he could and managed to stay ahead of the wolves for a mile or two but eventually they closed upon us. I broke a chair over the head of one wolf that jumped into the back of the wagon. Other wolves soon overtook us and they pulled Poky down. Several wolves converged upon me inside the wagon. I fought them off with cooking utensils, furniture and whatever else I could find. However, soon they were biting my arms and legs and I knew that the end was not far off.

Suddenly, there was a bright burst of white light so intense that I was temporarily blinded. When I regained my sight, the wolves were gone and I was staring at the most beautiful and peaceful face I had ever seen. Everything about her was white. She had fair skin, long straight hair and pointed ears. I stared into her deep blue eyes and felt the warmth and power of her presence.

She placed her hand over my eyes and said, "Rest, little one and do not fear for I will take care of you."

Willet paused for a moment before continuing.

"When I awoke, I was at the place I call home and to which I will now take you."

The rays of sunlight had left the cave and a gray twilight had settled in when Willet rose from his chair and said, "It is time for us to go. Please join hands with each other."

They formed a ring around the outside of the basin. The

water in the basin was as clear as glass. Willet began to chant some strange words and the water stirred and bubbled. A mist soon formed on the surface so Tom could no longer see the bottom of the basin.

"It is time," Willet said and he led them as they all stepped into the basin.

Tom felt a cold, damp sensation on his feet that slowly worked its way upward. It felt as though he was sinking until he was totally immersed in a gray mist. Although he could not see Willet or Wini, he continued to hold their hands which reassured him. Tom was about to speak when the mist suddenly lifted as though they had dropped out of a cloud. They were standing on a rocky path surrounded by snow-capped mountains. A short distance ahead, the path descended into a misty fog that formed a thick cloud bank surrounded by mountain peaks.

Willet smiled and said, "Welcome to my home."

He turned towards the pathway shrouded in mist and raised his arms as if in prayer. Closing his eyes he began to sing with a voice that seemed to rise from the depths of his being.

Tom was struck by the richness and beauty of Willet's singing which was quite unlike his speaking voice. Something inside Tom stirred and he was deeply moved. A presence that he had never felt before filled and then seemed to overflow his being. Suddenly, he too raised his arms and started to sing with Willet. He felt energized by a powerful force deep within him. Words in some unknown tongue flowed from his lips with such enthusiasm and power that Willet stopped singing. Willet and Wini looked at Tom with astonishment as he continued Willet's song as though he had sung it a hundred times before!

Suddenly, a female voice from within the mist joined Tom's singing in perfect harmony. As they sang together, the mist gradually disappeared to reveal a great chasm spanned by an arched bridge of crystalline ice. Other voices from the left and right of the bridge joined the singing. With each new voice, Tom felt a surge of energy, love and unity being expressed that he could not explain.

Willet's face beamed with radiant joy as he too rejoined the singing. Soon Wini and many others joined a swelling chorus that grew to thousands of voices.

The remaining mist rapidly evaporated to reveal a city of ice that glistened like diamonds in the waning rays of the sun. The city had towers and walls that emerged from the sheer rock face of a huge mountain on the far side of the chasm. Tom could see sentries posted on the walls and at the far end of the bridge.

Everywhere he looked people were singing with arms upraised while standing transfixed in exuberant praise. The ground shook from the powerful vibration of the song. Then, like a crashing wave, the song waned and everyone lowered their arms. Willet looked at Tom and slowly bowed while extending his arms with palms up. He then straightened up and crossed his arms placing his palms on his chest.

"Great blessings and grace have been poured out upon us," said Willet. "For you to have raised the mist and led in such a powerful song shows that you are on the path to become a son of light."

Willet paused and grew somber, "I must warn you that Devlin knows of your escape from Andhun and undoubtedly also felt the earth shake. Beware, for he will do all in his considerable power to deceive or destroy you."

"How?" asked Tom. "Am I not safe here with you and the elves?"

Willet replied, "You are safe here. However, the path that leads to becoming a son of light begins but does not end here. Come, an old friend approaches and we still have much to do before the night ends."

As they walked down the path towards the bridge, Tom could see a woman at the far end of the bridge approaching. She seemed to float towards them with elegance and grace. A faint white glow emanated from her tall and slender body. She wore a long white dress with a silver sash and slippers that blended perfectly with her long white hair and skin. She drew near as they reached the center of the bridge and Tom was struck by her beauty. She looked straight into Tom's eyes and he felt the same penetrating gaze that he experienced with Prince Caelin.

"Wes ou hal! Sir Egric! Long have I prayed for this meeting," she said as she bowed towards Tom in the same fashion as Willet had just done.

Willet said, "He calls himself Tom."

"As you wish," replied the lady.

"This is Linette, princess of the elves who inhabit the high places of the earth," said Willet as he bowed towards her.

"My heart leaps for joy at our reunion!"

Willet placed his hand on Wini's shoulder as he said, "This is Wini, shepherd of the plains of Redwald."

Wini became flushed with embarrassment and did not know what to say. He attempted to bow like Willet but was awkward and uneasy in the presence of a woman of such beauty and nobility.

"You are all most welcome!" said Princess Linette. "Tom, will you accompany me?"

Now it was Tom's turn to be flustered which drew sweet laughter from the princess.

"Please take my hand. There is nothing to fear," she said as she extended her hand.

Tom was unsure of what to do and looked instinctively towards Willet who grabbed his hand and placed it on top of hers. They proceeded to the city with Willet and Wini following. As they approached the main gate, the princess began to sing a joyful song and, once again, the others joined in. This time, Tom was content to listen to the song which was incomprehensible but pleasant.

Willet leaned forward and whispered in Tom's ear "The elves are rejoicing with a song in your honor."

As they entered the city, Tom could see that there were thousands of elves lining the main street. As they passed, the elves on both sides would bow as Willet and the princess had done as a sign of honor and welcome. They continued into the city until they came to a large palatial building in the center. They proceeded up the steps and into a great hall filled with elves.

As they crossed the hall on a white marble floor, Tom was amazed at the height of the ceiling and the massive rows of columns on either side. At the far end of the hall, marble stairs lead to a platform with a circular table surrounded by twelve chairs. Light beams from the last rays of the sun illuminated the table from above. They stopped when they reached the bottom of the steps leading to the platform,

There was complete silence as thousands of elves watched with anticipation.

Willet gave Tom and Wini a reassuring smile and motioned for them to face each other. Willet whispered, "Trust and obey for you are being honored before this assembly."

"Please join hands and kneel," said Princess Linette as she took a vial from a nearby pedestal and poured its contents onto the heads of Tom and Wini. She stood behind Tom and Willet moved behind Wini. They joined their right hands while placing their left on the back of the heads of Tom and Wini. Tom looked at Wini and forced a nervous smile in response to the apprehensive look on his face.

"Please close your eyes," said Princess Linette.

After a brief pause, the Princess and Willet began to hum a song that seemed to vibrate through Tom and Wini until they were all resonating in unison. Tom felt a warm tingling sensation at the back of his head where the Princess was touching him. This sensation moved down his spine and throughout his body. Tom felt a flow of energy into his body that became progressively stronger until it overpowered his senses and he became dizzy. He struggled to maintain his balance but the dizziness increased until he finally had to open his eyes to stabilize himself.

Tom stared in fear and amazement at the scene before his eyes. "I must be dreaming or hallucinating," he said to himself.

Tom was looking down at himself and the others as though he was floating! Suddenly, Wini appeared next to him. "Wini, are you OK?"

"Yes Master Tom," he replied and asked, "Are we dreaming?"

"What you see is quite real," replied a familiar voice as Willet appeared.

"What you are experiencing is called astral projection. It is the ability to separate mind and soul from the body while remaining conscious and cognizant of the surroundings."

Willet continued, "This is your initiation into the spiritual realm. I will train you further, but this is enough for your first experience. Take my hand and we shall return."

As soon as Tom touched Willet's hand, he felt like he was falling back into his body. The next thing he knew he was looking at Wini's excited face.

"WOW!" Wini exclaimed. "That was fantastic! I feel like a blind man who can now see!"

Tom smiled and gave Wini a hug. "I am very happy you are with me to share in these strange and wonderful new experiences!"

Princess Linette said, "Rise so that I may present you to my people."

Tom and Wini turned towards the elves as Princess Linette said, "Never before in our history has a human stirred the spirit of the Creator in us as we have experienced this day. Even the earth resonated in unison and bore witness to the movement of the Creator!"

Tom glanced up at her face as she spoke and thought he had never seen such a beautiful sight.

She beamed with joy and light seemed to glow from her face as she continued, "Are these not the first signs that have been foretold in the prophecies regarding the coming of the sons of light? Even now, you have seen how easily they have transcended to the spirit realm."

She raised her arms and looked around at the assembly as she proclaimed, "From henceforth let this day be remembered as the dawn of the sons of light that we have long awaited! Let us rejoice and be diligent to love and serve as we have been commanded to hasten the fulfillment of the prophecies."

The elves responded with an enthusiastic shout, "So be it! We shall trust and obey!" After a mighty cheer that lasted several minutes, the elves dispersed.

WILLET'S HOME

*W*ILLET BOWED TOWARDS PRINCESS LINETTE who returned the gesture. Then he turned towards Tom and said, "Come, I will show you to my house."

He led Tom and Wini through a side door near the platform and out into the street, which was filled with happy and excited elves returning to their homes.

"Master Tom! Over here!"

Tom turned to see Cearl and another elf working their way through the crowd towards them.

"Cearl!" Tom shouted and likewise moved through the crowd towards him. When they reached each other, Cearl attempted to bow but Tom gave him a hug, which embarrassed and pleased Cearl.

Tom asked, "What happened to you?"

Willet replied, "Before you answer that question, let's continue to my house, which is just down the street. I sense that this will be a story best told over dinner, which my stomach says is long overdue."

Tom was so preoccupied by the events of the day that he had not thought about eating. However, at the mention of food, there was unanimous agreement to proceed to Willet's house. As they continued, Cearl introduced the elf who was with him.

"This is Penda, who has been assigned to Wini by Prince Caelin."

After a short walk, they arrived at a modest-looking cottage that Tom noticed was similar in appearance to Willet's house in Downs End. There was smoke coming from the chimney and yellow light flickered in the windows. Willet opened the door to reveal a small room with simple, wooden furniture. The warmth from the fireplace and a large candle on the table gave the room a cozy feeling.

There was a table and five chairs near the hearth, which contained a pot of some sort of stew. Each place at the table was set with care, and there were various sorts of fruit, fresh baked breads, and vegetables on the table. The scent of old books competed with the aromas of stew and bread. The smell of old books also reminded him of Willet's home in Downs End. He wondered if there was a reading room through the only other doorway, which was closed.

Willet remarked, "It appears that Princess Linette has anticipated our hunger and has made arrangements for our dinner. Please sit down and I will serve up some stew."

Once they were seated and served, Willet looked at Tom and said, "After Cearl found me and reported that you had lost the path, we searched for you. After several hours we decided to split up. Cearl retraced the path to the lake while I returned to our meeting place by the waterfall. I found evidence of your arrival, which led me to conclude that you must have entered the portal in the pool. When I looked into the pool I could see Andhun's banquet room, but I could not enter as there was a saber tooth tiger at the entrance. I had previously studied this portal and knew that it was unstable and could close at any time so I decided to remain at the entrance and try to hold it open as long as possible. I sent an urgent message to Cearl, who contacted Wini, which resulted in your escape."

Tom asked, "How did you contact Cearl and why did Cearl warn Wini instead of me?"

Willet laughed and said, "I am glad I decided to keep my story brief or I would be spending the rest of the night answering your questions!"

"Cearl contacted Wini because your mind was closed to the possibility that you were in danger, while Wini was sensing it."

"The answer to your first question requires an introduction and some concentration."

Willet closed his eyes and placed his hands together on the table with his palms up. His lips began to move but no sound came out. Tom heard a faint sound like a wind chime that gradually got louder until a small, bright light entered the room through a crack under the front door. The light buzzed around the room several times and came to rest in Willet's open hands.

Willet opened his eyes and said, "Let me introduce a dear friend of mine. Etain, please show yourself. I would like you to meet Tom and Wini."

The brightness of the light diminished to reveal a miniature woman with elfish features and wings dressed in a long white robe similar to Princess Linette. She smiled and bowed but remained silent. Willet explained, "Etain is of the race of fairies who, like the elves, are descendants of the Aigneis that remained faithful to the Creator."

Tom asked "Why is she so small and why doesn't she speak?"

Willet replied, "Double questions again, Master Tom! I fear I will be overwhelmed with questions once your formal training begins! I will answer and then Cearl will give his report."

"The fairies are of the same race as the elves but different in stature and with wings. They communicate only telepathically, which will be part of your training.

"Now, please Cearl, give us your report, and let's have no more questions until he is done."

Willet Summons Etain

BATTLE FOR THE DARACH TREES

THE ROOM WAS SILENT EXCEPT for the occasional crackling of wood in the fireplace. Everyone stared expectantly at Cearl, who leaned backwards in his chair and closed his eyes.

A troubled look appeared on his face and, after collecting his thoughts, he opened his eyes and said, "After we parted I followed the path back to the enchanted lake without seeing any sign of Master Tom. It was dusk when I reached the lake so I decided to visit my father to see if he could offer any advice. I passed through the portal and arrived in the Valley of Glainne. Upon my arrival, I was dismayed to find my kinsfolk scurrying about and so I asked someone hurrying past me what was happening."

"Enemy forces are massing along the western woodlands. Prince Caelin has ordered all warriors to the perimeter defenses."

I made haste to the western woodlands to meet my father at the main command post. I knew that our scouts had recently reported that there was an army of orcs assembling in the woodlands a day's march to the west of the border. However, it was thought that they were still dispersed and would not be at full strength for several more weeks. I ran as fast as I could and soon found my father inside the main chamber of a large darach tree, which served as a command post for the perimeter defenses. He was surrounded by elf lords who were gathered around a large table with a map.

"What is a darach tree?" blurted Wini.

Willet looked sternly at Wini, which caused him to mouth a silent apology.

Cearl on the other hand smiled and did not seem to mind the interruption. He explained, "Darach trees are the oldest living creatures of the forest. They are thousands of years old and were planted by the first elves to inhabit the land. Their bark is thick and fire resistant. They have deep roots that can rapidly move large quantities of water to their leaves and grow to over one hundred feet tall. Their diameter at the base is typically fifty feet and they are hollow inside. With holes for windows in their trunks and battlements added to their branches they make formidable fighting towers. Sentinel darach trees are scattered throughout the forest but a continuous line of them form the primary defensive perimeter about a mile into the forest."

"Thank you Cearl," said Willet as he scowled at Tom and Wini.

"Please continue."

Cearl nodded and said, "As soon as I entered the room where my father was meeting with the other elf lords, he looked up, rushed over to me, and gave me a warm embrace while asking, 'Are you well?'"

"'I am well but I have been separated from Master Tom.'"

Prince Caelin replied, "It is a blessing to see you despite the evil tide of events that are about to overtake us. I fear that death will part many friends this night. Let's pray for Tom's safety even as we prepare for the battle before us."

The Prince continued, "The werewolves that pursued you last night must have brought word of Tom's escape to the nearby orcs. They have marched quickly and are rapidly assembling along the river. Our scouts say that there are at least twenty thousand orcs supported by hundreds of cave trolls and werewolves."

I looked at the map and could see orc symbols forming a line several miles long on the opposite side of the river. In addition, there were many other groups of orc symbols dispersed around the river that indicated that they were still gathering reinforcements. I knew that their opposition was not more than five thousand elves.

As if sensing my thoughts, Prince Caelin said, "We have sent for help from our nearest kinsfolk, but I do not think they will arrive before the attack begins."

Rubbing his chin with his hand he continued as though talking to himself, "Although we are relatively few, we are well hidden. Furthermore, their haste to find and destroy Tom can be to our advantage, for they are forcing this fight without first consolidating all of their forces."

Suddenly, many warning horns sounded from the right and the left announcing the beginning of the battle. A few seconds later the tower shook from a powerful collision. The elf lords around the table quickly dispersed to their posts.

Prince Caelin said, "They have catapults!"

Turning to the spiral staircase leading up the tower he shouted to me, "Stay close to me!"

The night sky was ablaze with hundreds of yellow lights that emerged from the woods beyond the river. They appeared to jump up from the forest in the distance like swarms of fireflies. As they approached, they grew larger until they turned into flaming boulders that crashed into the surrounding forest with great force and destruction.

When they hit the trees, showers of flames sprayed from them starting a hundred fires along the path of each boulder. Already there were fires burning in many places. Numerous elves were hurrying through the trees or on the ground to avoid or put out the fires.

Prince Caelin and I watched as an elf near the base of our tree ran to a nearby well and drew a bucket of water. The elf threw the water onto one of the many flames on the forest floor. Instead of extinguishing the fire, the water spread it.

Prince Caelin looked with alarm at the rapidly spreading flames and said, "This is no ordinary fire! It is Teidich! Cursed flames from the abyss! Sound the retreat! Pull back to the darach trees!"

The sentinel next to the Prince sounded his horn, which echoed through the forest as the elves withdrew.

The continuous rain of fireballs from across the river soon turned the forest into an inferno. Ten foot tall trolls rolled boulders in pitch and set them ablaze using lamps carrying fire from the abyss deep within the earth. The intensity of the fire burned up the forest by morning, leaving a charred wasteland of contorted tree trunks. Scattered among the blackened remains of the forest were darach trees that survived by producing a steady rain of water from their leaves. One mile from the river, another line of darach trees stood like a wall that kept the fire from spreading further into the forest.

A thick smoky haze covered the scorched earth where a lush green forest had stood the previous day. The bright yellow blaze of the previous evening had given way to the flickering red glow of thousands of embers marking what remained of large tree trunks. A light rain began to fall, which increased the smoky haze until it settled like a thick blanket on the ground and prolonged the twilight before dawn.

I was among the scouts who moved like ghosts among the wreckage of the forest near the river assessing the position and strength of the orcs as well as the damage to the defenses. Most of the pits and trenches lined with wooden stakes were exposed or badly damaged. The thick haze allowed me and several hundred other elves to approach the river unseen and send harassing volleys of arrows into the assembling orc ranks. The orcs countered by sending hundreds of werewolves across the river. The other scouts and I withdrew and enticed many werewolves to their deaths by showing ourselves to them on the far side of some of the still-hidden traps.

"'Boom! Boom! Boom!"

The air vibrated as hundreds of orc kettledrums beat in unison along the river. The ground shook as twenty thousand orcs advanced in cadence to the booming drums. These orcs were well organized and disciplined in their tactics. They formed two waves about two hundred paces apart that stretched over three miles long. Each wave consisted of similarly armed orcs organized into five ranks: two lines of orcs wielding spears followed by a line each of those brandishing axes, those brandishing swords, and archers.

Trolls brought up the rear pulling the catapults that had fired the flaming boulders the previous night. They slowly moved in unison to the beat of the drums, which helped them stay organized as they crossed the smoke-filled wasteland. Occasionally, parts of the first rank would disappear into a trench or pit but such gaps were quickly filled by orcs from the sides or rear so that their ranks were reformed and they continued to advance.

The drums suddenly stopped when the first rank of orcs was just beyond the reach of the archers in the darach tree perimeter. The orcs stood in their ranks while the trolls set up the catapults to bombard the forest beyond the darach tree perimeter. Soon the forest on the far side of the darach tree perimeter was ablaze from the flaming boulders. When it was clear that the elves were trapped in the darach trees between the orcs and the flames, the trolls concentrated the catapults on the battlements of the trees.

Prince Caelin and an elf lord named Lord Swefred surveyed the advance of the orcs from one of the battlements at the top of the command post tree. Lord Swefred was one of the largest of the elves and was renowned for his military skills.

"Lord Swefred, your division will reinforce the perimeter defenses until you hear my signal, then form ranks and move to your new position," commanded Prince Caelin.

Lord Swefred bowed and said, "May the Creator strengthen us and bring destruction on the destroyers!"

Prince Caelin smiled and said, "Be careful, old friend!"

Prince Caelin quickly moved down the spiral staircase in the trunk of the tree until he came to the map room on the ground level. He shifted the map table and the rug under it to reveal a trap door and another staircase that led to a tunnel beneath the command post tree.

The darach trees had an interconnected network of root tunnels that was used by elves during times like these. Prince Caelin led a thousand elves into these tunnels. Their destination was the sentinel trees beyond the orc lines. The sentinel darach trees were abandoned by the elves during the first forest fire and so were by-passed by the orcs, who concentrated on the darach perimeter trees.

"The trolls are three hundred feet away, Prince Caelin," whispered a scout.

"Very well. Pass the word to concentrate on the trolls first," replied Prince Caelin.

Although the haze was thick, the flaming boulders easily marked the positions of the trolls while enabling the elves to remain hidden. A thousand elf archers broke into groups, each targeting trolls working the catapults. Fairies flew between the elf groups assisting with communications.

When Prince Caelin received word from the fairies that all the groups were in position, he ordered the attack. A piercing horn blast signaled the launch of a thousand arrows, which killed or wounded most of the trolls. Seconds later, a second volley of arrows followed and finished the remaining trolls before they could raise an alarm.

"Elves advance! Double quick!" ordered Prince Caelin.

The elves quickly and quietly descended on the catapults and adjusted them to target the second orc wave. When all the catapults were ready, Prince Caelin ordered the attack and a second horn blast launched thousands of arrows and hundreds of flaming boulders into the second orc wave. The boulders tore huge holes into the orc lines while the flaming pitch showered them with flames.

Soon the second wave of orcs was consumed in flames. Those that escaped the flames broke ranks and ran wildly through the haze. Many of them were cut down by an advancing line of elves led by Prince Caelin. As they approached the wall of flames that marked the location of the second orc wave, Prince Caelin shouted, "Elves to the right double quick!"

The orcs in the first wave heard the screams and saw the flames through the haze where the second wave had been. Their commander, Crodha, pushed his way to the rear of the orc ranks and was filled with rage as he realized the quick turn of events. He knew their position would be targeted next so he ordered an assault on the darach perimeter thinking that the elves would not fire on the trees.

Ten thousand orcs and werewolves advanced on the darach perimeter with grappling hooks, ladders, and ropes. Although the elves in the trees fought valiantly, the sheer number of orcs enabled them to scale and enter the trees in numerous places and overwhelm the elves. Just when it appeared that the perimeter would be overrun, a third horn blast announced a change in the tide of the battle.

Crodha had entered the command post and was fighting for control when the third elf horn sounded. Looking out a tower window he could see that he was correct in his assumption that the catapults were not targeting the trees. However, he was dismayed to see that the flaming boulders were landing progressively closer producing a creeping wall of flames that approached the trees from the direction of the assault. On the opposite side of the perimeter trees, the forest blazed from the initial assault, trapping them between two walls of flames. What he had not anticipated and could not see through the haze was that his army was trapped between two thousand elves advancing against both of his flanks.

The haze of smoke hid the movements of the elves who had formed ranks at the flanks of the orc lines between the walls of flames. Once the third horn blast was sounded, Prince Caelin and Lord Swefred simultaneously ordered the advance against the orc flanks.

The sudden appearance of advancing ranks of elves, the surrounding flames, and the elves in the trees above caused confusion and panic among the orcs. They broke ranks and scattered into groups trying to find an escape from the trap. Some ran into the flames hoping to pass through before they caught on fire. Prince Caelin and Lord Swefred both made their way steadily towards the center of the orc army, further constricting the trap.

When Crodha became aware of the trap, he rallied his troops against Lord Swefred's division hoping to break through. Under his command, the orcs regained their organization and fell upon Lord Swefred's division, driven by determination and desperation. Although their numbers had been greatly reduced, three thousand fanatic orcs and werewolves advanced like a wave upon less than one thousand elves.

Prince Caelin's division advanced like a threshing machine mowing down the disorganized and fleeing orcs. They were almost to the command post in the center when a frantic distress call was sounded in the distance ahead of them.

The elf horn blared loud and clear giving Prince Caelin reason to believe that Lord Swefred's division was in trouble.

"Advance double quick!" shouted Prince Caelin and they increased their pace.

Although Prince Caelin rushed to the sound of the distress call, he reached Lord Swefred's position too late. He found Lord Swefred in the midst of a pile of orcs and elves with a spear through his chest.

Willet groaned and Cearl clenched his teeth as he fought back tears. After he regained his composure, he continued.

While most of the orc army had been destroyed, a few hundred orcs managed to breach the elf line and then broke into small groups to escape through the haze. Crodha led one such group in a wide circle that would return them to the orc camp. He had failed to defeat the elves and capture or kill the human lad that had been born into their world. However, he still hoped to salvage his life and honor by presenting his master with an elf-stone that he had taken from the elf lord that he had killed.

"This is most grievous news!" exclaimed Willet.

"What did Prince Caelin do?"

Cearl replied, "My father immediately ordered the pursuit of the escaped orcs based on the number and size of their trails leading from the battle field. Hundreds of fairies dispersed into the haze to search for the fleeing orcs. While I was tracking down these orcs, Etain found me and brought your message regarding the danger that Tom and Wini were facing from Andhun. I immediately hurried to warn Wini in his dreams. Fortunately, Wini heeded my warning and helped Tom escape from Andhun. I was then instructed by my father to help you and Tom recover Lord Swefred's seeing stone."

Cearl's report weighed heavily upon Willet. Tom noticed

tears form in the corners of his eyes at the mention of Lord Swefred's death. Willet closed his eyes and sat in silence for several minutes as if in prayer or deep thought.

Willet whispered, "Farewell, Lord Swefred, dear friend, until we meet again at the end and the beginning of all things."

He opened his eyes and looked at the fairy.

"Etain, please inform Princess Linette of these events and seek her counsel."

"Master Tom, I fear that we must accelerate your training in order to locate this elf-stone."

Tom asked, "Why is this stone so important?"

Willet looked at him and Tom saw fear in his eyes. Willet nervously stroked his beard and said, "It is one of the twelve destined for the sons of light."

MIN

The BLAST OF THE GIANT tsuga horn jolted Min from a restless sleep. The smell of smoke was stifling and a steady, cold rain was falling. He was cold and wet and his muscles ached from the intense effort of launching scores of flaming boulders the previous night. As he stood he slipped on the muddy ground and felt depressed as he realized that even more work would be required today to move and work the catapult.

"Get up you lazy worms!" shouted the troll master.

His whip made a cracking sound and lashed the head of one of the dozing trolls next to Min.

Each catapult was tended by five trolls: two pushed the catapult and two pulled a cart of boulders while another pulled a pitch cart. Pulling the pitch carts was the least desirable position as it was a hot and smelly business with the potential for getting burned if the pitch spilled out of the large iron pot. Each catapult crew was lead by a troll master who carried a lamp containing the teidich fire.

Min grabbed the rope harness for the pitch cart and wrapped it around his waist and shoulders. Although he was not quite fully grown, he was stronger than most adult trolls. While he did his best to serve, his demeanor was gentle, which was so unusual among trolls that he was thought to be mentally deficient.

Min noticed that the rain was extinguishing the remnants of the forest fire they had caused the previous night. The thickening haze made the orcs in the battle lines in front of him look like shadows. His eyes burned from the smoke and he fought the urge to cough, which would be considered a sign of weakness.

Once the orcs and trolls formed ranks, they stood still awaiting the slow methodical beat of the giant kettledrums. Min tried to look fierce and determined like the other trolls, but inside he was wishing this battle would end soon so he could eat and get out of this miserable, wet weather.

He had never been in a battle before and, so far, it was not the glorious business that the others had told him about. It was hard work pulling carts and loading boulders into the catapult. While the flaming boulder barrage and the resulting forest fire were impressive, the resulting charred and hazy wasteland created a feeling of loss within him.

"Boom! Boom! Boom!"

With every beat, the ground shook as they stepped in unison. The power of the unified movement of the orcs made Min feel proud to be a part of something much larger than himself. After a short distance, Min heard a loud crack and the cart he was pulling suddenly got impossibly heavy. He turned and saw that the axle on the cart was broken and the front end had pushed up a wall of mud that partially buried it.

"Damn the luck!" cursed the troll master when he saw the damage.

Turning to the others he shouted, "Keep the beat! We can still throw boulders at them!"

Then he looked at Min and said, "I suppose I should be grateful that the loss is minimal."

With a snarl and a lash from his whip that brought a trickle of blood from a cut on Min's neck, he said, "Prove that you are not a worthless slacker by fixing the axle and rejoining us before we use up all of our boulders."

"Aye, Sir," replied Min as he removed the harness and pushed the cart out of the mud. He quickly verified that the lid of the pitch pot was secure and rolled it off the cart. Then he turned and stared as the trolls slowly disappeared into the haze. The grayness seemed to envelope them until they vanished as though they no longer existed. Although he could hear the drums and feel their footsteps, a feeling of separation and loss overwhelmed him and he struggled to not run after them.

"I must hurry and repair the axle so that I can rejoin them with honor," he mumbled to himself.

He tried to control his fear by focusing on replacing the axle. By the time he removed the broken axle and went to find a replacement, the sound of drums had receded and then stopped completely, which enhanced his sense of loneliness.

"Be brave, Min, there's nothing to fear," he told himself.

As he walked through the nearby woods looking for a branch or tree trunk to match the size of the axle, he contemplated his loneliness. He was separated from his parents soon after birth, in keeping with the custom of the trolls. Emotional attachments were detrimental to the goals set for them by Devlin as well as the collective good of the troll population.

His parents were strangers who were paired by a shaman troll until he was born and then they were separated. He had rotated among groups of trolls every few years to learn the troll values of obedience and team work while avoiding the emotional attachments that led to envy, selfishness, and strife.

He had been raised in the proper troll manner, so why did he feel like something was missing? Why did he secretly desire to have a friend?

"Maybe there is something wrong with me," he muttered.

The strange sound of an elf horn shook him from his thoughts. He stopped and turned toward the battlefield. He could see a distant glow of another forest fire through the haze. A multitude of indistinguishable sounds told him that the battle had been joined in earnest.

"I wonder what the elves look like," he said to himself.

He had been told that elves were a deceitful and arrogant race that rebelled against Devlin. Every troll knew that the elves had to be either conquered or destroyed before the kingdom of peace and prosperity promised by Devlin could be established.

He found a suitable tree to replace the cart axle and started cutting it down with the axe he took from the pitch cart. He cringed when a second elf horn sounded.

"I wonder what is happening," he muttered to himself. "What happened to the tsuga horns and kettle drums?"

He struggled to suppress a growing sense of dread that the battle was not going well.

"I must hurry. They may need my help," he told himself.

Soon he felled the tree and removed the branches. He finished cutting the trunk to axle length and was carrying it back to the cart when another elf horn sounded. Min could no longer suppress his fear and he ran on the muddy ground, sliding and falling before reaching the cart. He had just finished repairing it when a group of orcs suddenly emerged from the haze in the direction of the river.

"Fall in you maggot!" commanded their leader.

"We'll need every able-bodied warrior to escape. They are not done with us yet."

Min fell in behind the commander and they started to run north parallel to the river. He was pleased that the orc commander had called him a warrior but he also was ashamed that he had not helped in the battle.

Min noticed one of the orcs running near him was bleeding profusely from an arrow in his side and was laboring to keep the pace. Min felt sorry for him so he grabbed the orc and lifted him onto his back. As he ran, he could feel the blood from the wound soaking into his clothes.

"Hold on! We will make it together!" he yelled to the orc on his back.

They seemed to be blindly plunging into an endless wall of gray haze. Min could not see more than twenty feet ahead and he began to wonder if their leader knew where he was going. He asked an orc running beside him who their leader was.

"Are you dense? Don't you know Crodha?"

Min was shocked at this revelation. He had never seen

Crodha but he knew his name and that he was the commander of their army. Min felt a knot in his stomach as he realized that, if Crodha was leading their escape, then a catastrophe must have befallen his people.

Suddenly, several small, yellow lights emerged from the haze and then quickly disappeared.

"Fairies! We've been spotted!" Crodha shouted.

"Sharp turn to the left! We'll have to loose them in the forest!"

Crodha decided to change direction to throw off the pursuing elves. He opted against continuing on the most direct escape route in favor of entering the woods, where he knew there was a lake that they could use to cover their tracks by wading through it or hiding in it if necessary.

A short distance after entering the woods they reached the shore of the lake. Before Crodha could give any orders, the trees around them started to explode and fall as huge boulders crashed around them. An elf horn sounded and a shower of arrows rained upon them. The orcs around him began to scatter and fall as arrows seemed to sprout around him.

Min jumped over fallen orcs and dodged falling trees until his legs felt numb and he gasped for air. A large shadow suddenly appeared on the ground and he looked over his shoulder just as a tree fell onto him.

Min slowly opened his eyes and tried to focus on where he was. The triple image of a daisy several feet from his face gradually consolidated into one image. He had a splitting headache and his tongue was swollen from thirst. A stifling weight pressed down on his back making it hard to breathe. He noticed that he could move his arms and legs but he seemed to be immersed in mud. Then he remembered the falling tree and the orc on his back. He slowly began to work his way back and forth in the muck until he slid himself out from under the tree. The orc on his back was dead. Min thought that it was ironic that, in trying to save the orc, he had probably saved his own life.

Still dazed by the knock from the tree, he sat and surveyed the area. Everywhere he looked, there were blasted and broken trees, weapons, and the bodies of orcs. Min noted the absence of any elves and told himself that the battle had either been a massacre or the elves had retrieved their casualties. In either case, he knew that the elves had won and could still be in the area. He slowly rose to his feet and staggered towards the lake. When he reached the shore he threw himself into the water and enjoyed the soothing coolness and cleansing action of the lake.

He worked his way into deeper water until he was up to his neck. After he had satisfied his thirst, he continued to wade in the deeper water moving parallel to the shore until he was a good distance away.

"At least they won't be able to track me," he thought. A few times he sank below the surface but quickly moved towards shallow water.

"Must be careful because trolls sink and can't swim," he reminded himself.

"It will be dark soon and then I will return to shore."

After a short distance, he noticed an orc floating in the water. As he approached, he was shocked to see that it was

Crodha. Apparently, he had tried to escape by entering the lake but an elf archer had put an arrow through his neck.

Min began to push the body away when he noticed a faint glow in the water nearby. He reached into the water to grab the source of the glow and, much to his surprise, he pulled Crodha's clenched fist out of the water. In it was a smooth, elliptical shaped stone on a leather necklace.

Min was struck by the simplistic beauty of the stone. He decided to put it on and tucked it under his shirt. He continued moving through the water until it became too dark to see the shore. Min waded ashore and crawled into a thicket, where he soon fell sound asleep.

Min Finds Seeing Stone

NIGHT FLIGHT

"ONCENTRATE, MASTER TOM! YOU MUST focus!"

Tom's gaze was locked onto the scene below in which he saw Willet standing behind him with his hand on his head just as he had previously seen him in the great elf hall. Cearl was standing in front of him and had his hands on Tom's forehead while Tom was seated in a chair.

He heard a familiar voice ask, "Master Tom, are you all right?"

Tom looked towards the source of the voice and saw Cearl's spirit floating next to him.

"Of course he is all right," replied Willet.

"I understand that this is all a bit overwhelming but there is no time for careful training. Circumstances demand that we be reckless."

Willet grabbed Tom and looked into his eyes, "It is imperative that you do precisely as I say. Do you understand?"

Tom felt as light as a feather. A strange mixture of

exhilaration and fear came over him as he looked at Willet and nodded his head.

"Hold tightly to our hands no matter what happens!" commanded Willet.

"You are about to experience many strange, wonderful, and terrifying things that I don't have time to explain. We must make haste to find the missing seeing stone. Please place your seeing stone inside your shirt and don't take it out unless told to do so.

"Cearl, can we get there without passing through any active portals?"

"Yes, if we don't take the most direct route. However, this route will take us past two unstable portals that have been inactive for many days."

"Very well," replied Willet. "Let's proceed as quickly as possible."

Cearl grabbed Tom's other hand and they proceeded to fly at tremendous speed through the walls of the building and out into the star filled night sky. Tom closed his eyes when they flew into the wall but he passed through without any sensation. When he opened his eyes, he quickly closed them when he realized that they were hundreds of feet up in the air!

Gradually, he realized that he was safe in the grasp of Cearl and Willet, so he dared himself to keep his eyes open. Once he did so, he was captivated by the awesome beauty of the experience. The blackness of the evening sky was pin-cushioned with a million points of light. Below them lay jagged, snow-capped mountains, fir forests and silver lakes and streams.

Tom was thrilled by the beauty of this new perspective of the world, but he also had the uneasy feeling that he had been here before. He looked at Willet and then at Cearl. He was surprised to see that they were both armed with swords beneath their hooded cloaks, which covered them from head to toe. Cearl stared intently ahead, concentrating on the speed, height, and direction of their flight.

As Tom studied his features, Cearl looked at him with a knowing smile and said, "Do you remember this place? We have flown here many times before in your dreams!"

While Tom remembered having had some dreams about flying, he could not recall this particular place. Indeed, he could not recall flying so quickly and with such ease.

As if sensing his thoughts, Willet said, "Your unaided flying skills have not developed yet, which is why we are towing you."

"Trouble ahead!" shouted Cearl as he pointed below. "One of the portals appears to be active!"

Tom saw two small lakes a short distance ahead. One reflected the silver starlight but the other had an unnatural yellow glow. The surface of this lake suddenly erupted into a fountain with two levels. The upper level was smaller and shot up into the sky, splitting into two divergent arms that spread to the north and south.

As they approached, Tom could see that the upper fountain consisted of a multitude of human and elf spirits. Each human spirit appeared to be towed, much as Tom was, by one or two elf spirits. The lower level consisted of an even greater number of human spirits but these were unescorted and were running, hopping, and crawling in a bubbling mass that spread out over the surrounding countryside.

Willet looked worried and said, "We must make haste! There will soon be a convergence!"

They had just joined the southward flow of human and elf spirits when Cearl said, "Here they come!"

On the horizon ahead, Tom could see a white glow that gradually morphed itself into thousands of elf spirits speeding towards them.

Willet pointed to the right and left and shouted, "We must reach the elves ahead before the demons close upon us!"

Looking to either side Tom could see a red glow that resolved itself into thousands of demon spirits approaching from the east and west. They were about to be engulfed in a maelstrom of battling spirits!

"We are almost there!" shouted Cearl.

"Not soon enough! Dive for the trees!" ordered Willet.

They dove downward with such velocity that Tom became dizzy and started to loose consciousness. The ground seemed to expand and enlarge with frightening speed. Just as Tom thought they would plunge into the ground, they made a sharp turn and flew at treetop level. Tom looked up and saw the convergence of thousands of human, elf and demon spirits form into a dark cloud. He saw flashes of light and heard rumbling sounds from the force of the impact. The larger demons battled the elves for control of their human companions while the smaller ones descended upon the lower fountain of strictly human spirits.

Cearl looked up and shouted, "We've got company!"

Tom could see a group of demons break from the cloud and start to perform the same dive that they had just completed.

"There are too many of them to fight," said Willet.

"I agree. We'll have to try to outrun them," replied Cearl.

The trio streaked across the forest treetops at tremendous

speed with the demons in pursuit. The ground passed beneath them in a blur and Tom's eyes watered from the force of their flight. However, the demons steadily closed the distance between them.

Tom looked back and could see the expressions on the faces of the lead demons. Their cat-like eyes glowed red and they extended their arms towards them. Their clawed fingers opened and closed, grasping for them. Some grinned with evil delight, revealing large fangs. They had a look of eager expectation that they would soon win this race.

Just ahead, Tom could see a large lake. As they passed over it he noticed a river and charred forest beyond.

"It's no good!" shouted Willet. "We must buy some time!"

Cearl looked at Willet and gave him a wink. They suddenly dove into the lake below and changed directions underwater. By the time the demons dove into the water, they had emerged again and resumed their rush towards the charred forest. In the few seconds it took for the demons to figure out what had happened, they were far enough away that Tom could no longer see their faces. However, he did hear a collective shout of rage as the demons coalesced and resumed their pursuit.

As if in answer to their shout, an elf horn sounded and a hundred elf spirits emerged from the darach trees ahead. They formed a wedge shaped cloud that hurdled straight at them. As they approached, Tom saw Prince Caelin at the head of the formation. He was shining from head to toe in armor and carried a brilliant sword and shield. As the elves shot past just below them, Tom caught a glimpse of the Prince's face, which was both reassuring and frightening in its splendor and ferocity.

"We are safe for the moment," said Willet. "Nevertheless, we must hurry before the evening wanes."

A short distance ahead they descended onto the site of Lord Swefred's death. Orc bodies had been piled and were burning, while the elf casualties had been removed and buried. Weapons were still scattered about where their owners had fallen.

Cearl took them to the largest heap of weapons and said, "This is where Lord Swefred was killed."

Turning towards Tom, Willet said, "Please take out your seeing stone. You must lead us from here."

Tom took the seeing stone out and noticed that it had the same glow as when he had gone through the enchanted forest. While this was encouraging, he did not know what to do. He felt hopelessly inadequate to lead them.

As if reading his thoughts, Cearl said, "Remember what you learned in the enchanted forest. You don't have to know the way, just trust and obey."

Cearl's words caused a warm sensation in Tom's heart and he felt encouraged and strengthened.

Willet asked, "Do you see anything unusual?"

Tom looked around but did not see anything until he looked at the place where Lord Swefred had fallen. He rubbed his eyes and blinked several times as if trying to clear his vision.

He pointed to the ground nearby and said, "There is something there! That is where the body of Lord Swefred must have been! It has a faint glow like the image of the sun leaves on the inside of your eyelids after you look at it."

"Excellent!" exclaimed Willet. "Get closer to the image. What do you see?"

Tom walked over to Lord Swefred's last resting place and said, "The glow elongates into a faint streak of light that becomes visible in the light of the seeing stone!

"Wonderful!" shouted Willet. "Let's find where the trail ends."

Cearl and Willet took Tom's hands and they resumed their flight, but at a much slower pace. The trail appeared to be some sort of energy residue marking the passing of the stone. The trail rose from the ground to a height of about five feet and then headed towards the river. They followed the trail across the river and eventually into a lake. They then followed it in the lake until it led them to a thicket near the shore, where they found a sleeping troll.

"A troll has the stone! We must warn my father immediately!" shouted Cearl.

"One moment!" cautioned Willet. "I don't see the stone. Do you Master Tom?"

"No," replied Tom, "I see neither the stone nor the trail any longer."

"Then we must confirm that the troll has the stone," said Willet.

Turning to Cearl, Willet said, "Cearl, it is time to remove our cloaks."

"Wake him up!" commanded Willet.

Min was sound asleep when he heard a voice in his ear say, "Wake up! You have been discovered!"

Min instinctively jumped up and, with his heart pounding, he looked intently for the source of the voice but saw nothing. After a few minutes, he decided that the voice must have been part of a dream. He lay back down, closed his eyes and was about to return to sleep when the voice returned.

"The stone is gone! Someone has taken it!" said the voice.

Min jerked himself awake and sat up, instinctively pulling the stone from beneath his shirt. Min stared in astonishment at the glowing stone on his chest. The faint luster that he had seen when he found the stone was intensified so that he was temporarily blinded by the light when he looked at it. He felt a strange warmth deep inside from some energy source or presence.

"Look! The stone glows!" said the same voice from his dream.

Turning around Min saw three shining spirits, two of which were armed with swords and were dressed in brilliant amour. However, it was the middle one that seemed to fix Min's gaze, for it was wearing a glowing stone identical to his. Min had never seen such awesome and beautiful beings. He was awestruck and fell to the ground, covering his eyes with his hands.

After a moment, Min peeked between his fingers, and the tallest and oldest of the three spirits said, "Get up and don't be afraid. We will not harm you."

Min rose to his knees and shielded his eyes from the light around the three figures. He finally asked, "Who are you?"

"I am Willet, a wizard of the Order of Alastrine. This is Tom, son of Throm, and there is the elf Cearl."

"I must still be dreaming," Min mumbled to himself.

"I assure you that you are quite awake and that we are real persons, although what you see is but our spirits," said Willet.

"Humans and elves!" exclaimed Min. "How can this be? You are the most wonderful and beautiful beings I have ever seen. I have never seen humans or elves before, but I have been told that they are ugly, vile, and evil creatures."

"Nevertheless, we are as we appear," said Willet. "How did you come by the stone around your neck?" Willet asked suspiciously.

"I took it from a dead orc," replied Min.

"The stone was taken from an elf lord during the battle and does not belong to you," said Cearl. "You must return it!"

Min started to remove it from his neck when Willet said, "You cannot give us the stone in our present forms. Stay here until dawn and then follow the path shown to you by the light from the stone. Think of us as you follow the path shown by the stone and we shall meet next in person. You must remain hidden from all except us. Trust neither men, orcs, elves, nor even trolls until we meet. Most creatures will try to kill you to have the stone. Do you understand?"

Min nodded his head but inside he was filled with conflicting thoughts and emotions. He was about to ask if they would look the same as they appeared now, but the trio vanished in the twinkling of an eye.

Cearl said, "I do not trust him. We should go immediately to my father."

"There is no time," replied Willet. "We must hurry! Dawn approaches! Besides there is something strange happening that needs further study. It troubles me that the stone glows so brightly around the neck of the troll."

Cearl replied, "Not even the greatest of the elf lords can use the seeing stones. We are but care takers of them until the sons of light are revealed."

"Quite true!" said Willet. "I must look further into this

and consult Princess Linette once we have recovered the stone."

As they resumed their return flight Tom noticed that the sky in the east had changed from black to a light gray. The sky was strangely empty of any elves or demons. As they approached the portal that had activated on their outward journey, Tom could see the fountain of human spirits on the ground below. However, instead of spreading outwards, they were converging on the portal. Tom thought the scene below looked like water flowing down a drain.

"Why do they hurry back to the portal?" asked Tom.

"Dawn marks the end of dreams. Those who do not return die in their sleep," said Willet.

"How can this be? asked Tom.

Willet smiled at him and replied, "To dream of death as when evil spirits torment dreams does not result in death for the spirit returns to the body. However, if the werewolves would have killed your body, you would have died. Death also results when the spirit is separated from the body and unable to return as when the portal closes."

"Dawn marks the end of dreams," added Cearl.

"Then we must hurry!" urged Tom.

"Quite so!" stated Willet as they accelerated to an incredible speed, and soon returned to Willet's house.

MIN'S JOURNEY

*M*IN TOSSED AND TURNED UNTIL twilight announced the new day. The image of the three spirits seemed incredibly real but their instructions seemed ridiculous. He kept thinking about his vision and the words "follow the path shown by the glowing stone."

Was he really in danger because of this stone?

"I must have been dreaming," he said to himself as he tried to convince himself to ignore the dream and keep to his plans to return to his country.

"Perhaps the blow from the tree falling on me caused me to imagine it."

However, the wonder and beauty of the vision was burned into his memory so that he could not ignore it. He tried to think of something else but it kept returning to his mind. He became angry with himself for not being able to control his thoughts.

When dawn arrived, he sat up and pulled the stone out from inside of his shirt. He was frightened and excited to see that it glowed with the same intense light he experienced in his vision. As he looked at the stone, the light began to focus into a beam that seemed to indicate a distinct path, just as the spirits had said. He became frightened and put the stone back inside his shirt, which made the light disappear.

"It could be a trick," he told himself.

"They may just have appeared to be beautiful to trick me into giving them the stone. I know nothing of elves and men, but have heard nothing but bad things about them my whole life. Why should I go to them and forsake my people and my home?" he wondered.

"The safe and logical thing to do would be to return to my homeland as I had planned."

He decided to immediately resume his homeward journey and ignore the advice of the spirits.

As he crept through the thicket away from the direction shown by the glow of the stone, the weight around his neck seemed to get heavier with each step. He again pulled the stone out and looking down at it, he noticed that it no longer glowed. He turned around to look back at the way he had just come and saw that the stone glowed brilliantly as before, showing a path back to where he had slept.

"It seems as though the stone has a mind of its own. It appears that I'll either have to leave it or trust in the path it is showing me."

As he debated with himself as to what to do, he suddenly had a strong feeling of approaching danger. He retreated back into his hiding place in the thicket. After a few minutes, Min heard the tromping and clattering sounds of the approach of a group of warriors. He stared intently towards the source of the sound and soon saw a hundred orcs and a score of werewolves emerge from the woods about one hundred yards away across an open field. They were running past him and towards the river.

"They must be one of the scattered groups of orcs that were hoping to join the battle that was lost yesterday," he said to himself.

"I must warn them that they are hurrying to their doom."

Min started to move out of the thicket but stopped and stared in shock as the orcs drew near. He was struck by how distorted, evil, and cruel they appeared. Their eyes glowed red and they foamed at the mouth like rabid animals lusting to kill. The werewolves also were ghastly and frightening to behold. As they ran past snarling and howling, Min could see their sharp fangs. He was repulsed by their foul odor, which seemed to envelope them like a cloud. Min rubbed his eyes and blinked several times as if trying to clear his vision but these orcs and werewolves were unlike any that he had ever seen. Their dress, weapons, and movements were familiar but they seemed to reek with malice that elicited both fear and loathing in Min.

As they passed by, Min heard a horn blast and fifty elves emerged from the forest in the path of the advancing orcs. In contrast to the orcs and werewolves, the elves were radiant in their armor. They moved at a trot towards the orcs in a "V" formation with precision and grace.

The orcs and werewolves paused when they heard the horn blast but gave a collective snarl and charged when they saw the relatively small group of elves that challenged them.

Just before the two groups converged, a second horn blast sounded and a hundred arrows flew from the woods opposite Min's hiding place. The volley of arrows blanketed the on-rushing orcs and werewolves creating confusion and killing or wounding half their numbers. Before they could regroup, the elves charged into the disorganized mass. A third horn blast announced the appearance of one hundred more elves from the woods on the flank of the remaining orcs and werewolves. These elves quickly encircled the remaining enemy and wiped them out within minutes.

Even though the battle quickly became a massacre, Min admired the tactics and professional fighting style of the elves in contrast to the crude and vicious style of the orcs and werewolves. Following the battle, Min watched the elves collect their dead and wounded. They placed the dead enemy into piles, which they set on fire, and then disappeared into the forest.

It was late afternoon when Min left the thicket. He cautiously followed the path shown by the stone. The path he was following seemed to meander but he soon realized that it was the way that afforded him the most concealment. As he walked in a dry, cobble-filled streambed, he felt a sense of peace despite not knowing his destination. He felt he was being guided by some unknown power, which gave him comfort.

The sun had set and the darkness was growing when Min reached a cluster of boulders and decided to rest for the night. He was thirsty, tired, and hungry.

"I don't care if the stone likes it or not, I am going to find some food and drink first thing in the morning," he promised himself as he squeezed between two boulders.

"I hope there is somewhere to lie down inside this rock pile," he complained as he proceeded to climb over and around the large rocks.

As if in answer to his complaint, a small grass clearing appeared in the midst of the boulders. A slow but steady trickle of water dripped from a crack in a boulder nearby and there were numerous plants growing in the clearing. Min recognized purple gorse berries and buntata plants, whose roots were edible.

"Well, this is certainly an amazing finish to a most unusual day!" he exclaimed as he proceeded to eat and drink.

As Min reflected on the events of the day, he marveled that so much had changed in such a short time. It seemed as if his whole life had been turned upside down and he felt confused and betrayed. Elves and men appeared to be good while orcs and werewolves were evil. How could this be?

If some of the truths that he had been taught since his earliest memories were lies, then where could he place his trust? Indeed, he worried about what other beliefs and customs would prove to be false in the days ahead.

"It's this stone!" he said to himself. "It changes my vision. Perhaps I would be better off without it."

He took it off and set it on a rock next to him.

The light in the stone was very faint but gained intensity as he moved his hand close as if to pick it up. There was purpose and power in the stone, but what was its source? What if it was evil and was distorting his view of things instead of showing him the errors of his beliefs?

As he wrestled with these thoughts, he remembered the beauty, peace, and sense of purpose that the stone had brought to his life. He picked up the stone and felt good about the way it responded by glowing brightly. He had the feeling that whatever or whoever was behind this stone accepted him and wanted to be close to him.

"Maybe this is some sort of trick or trap and the beauty it has revealed is a lie. However, if this is the truth, then this is the most wonderful and exciting experience of my life! I would rather have just one more day like the last one with the stone than live a long life without it!"

Having set his mind to continue to trust in the stone, he laid down on a bed of grasses he had prepared and was soon sound asleep.

THE SEARCH FOR MIN

*W*HILE THEY WERE GONE, ETAIN notified Princess Linette, who convened a counsel of elves at Willet's house. After Tom, Willet, and Cearl returned to their bodies, Willet described the events of their journey. At the mention of Lord Swefred's death, Willet paused and was temporarily overcome by emotion. There was a stunned silence for several minutes while the elves gathered their thoughts. Tom looked around the room and saw intense grief and anger on the faces of the elves.

"This is a most grievous and unexpected turn of events," said Princess Linette.

"We must retrieve the stone immediately!" exclaimed Lord Ceowulf.

"It is an abomination for this troll to have one of the sacred stones! There's no telling where he will go with it or what greater evil and mischief might occur if we do not get it back as soon as possible!"

"Aye!"

"Amen!"

"Make it so!"

The council was in an uproar as most of the elves stood and shouted their affirmation and enthusiastic agreement with Lord Ceowulf, who was one of the most respected of the elf lords. A warrior of renown and a leader whose counsel was highly regarded, he was nearly as powerful as Princess Linette.

Willet said, "Tom will lead us to recover the stone. He has seen the troll that has it. He has but to concentrate on them and his stone will lead us."

Princess Linette added, "The fairies have reported a great victory by Prince Caelin's forces. However, there continue to be many smaller skirmishes in the area. Speed and stealth will serve our cause best. A small group should accompany Tom."

"I will go!" shouted Wini.

"Prince Caelin has charged me with looking after Tom and it is my duty to not be separated from him."

"Master Tom is my student and as such I also must go," Willet said.

Cearl and Penda also said they were bound to go based on their ties to Tom and Wini.

"Very well," said Princess Linette.

"Are there any among the elf lords who feel compelled to go?"

"I will go!" said Lord Ceowulf.

"I feel a burden to avenge Lord Swefred and return the seeing stone to the elves."

Etain also appeared and offered her assistance.

"A company of seven is a heavenly number," said Princess Linette. "You must leave immediately and make haste to recover the stone. I shall send word to Prince Caelin to also search for the troll."

Within an hour, they were ready to leave. It was early morning and a crowd of elves gathered to bid them farewell. All eyes turned toward Tom, who was to lead them. Tom blushed with embarrassment and felt nervous. He looked at Willet, who merely smiled confidently at him and nodded. He then looked at Cearl, who simply said, "Remember to trust and obey."

Although Tom felt totally inadequate, he also sensed the power from the stone.

"We have been in this situation before," he said to the stone. "I will follow as you lead," he whispered.

He thought of the troll and the missing stone, and the glow from his stone showed the path immediately ahead.

"This way!" he said with confidence that he did not feel. He began to lead the small group to an unknown destination.

The path indicated by the stone followed roads and paths of the elves through mountain passes, secluded alpine valleys and hair raising arched bridges with frightening spans. It was a bright, cloudless day but there was a cool breeze blowing from the snow-capped peaks. Tom recognized some of the mountains that they had flown over the previous night and felt reassured that they were going in the right direction.

The mood of the search party was somber and they proceeded in silence for several hours, reflecting on the loss of Lord Swefred, the missing stone, and the uncertainties and dangers that were ahead. Tom was grateful for the silence as he feared that someone would comment or challenge his leadership especially when they came to a crossroad or fork in the path. Eventually, his focus shifted to the enchanted beauty of their surroundings. There were meadows sprinkled with colorful wildflowers, crystal clear lakes and bubbling streams, spectacular waterfalls, and thick pine forests. Everywhere were the sounds of birds, insects, and occasional elvish songs from invisible sources.

Cearl moved beside Tom and proudly said, "These lands are called the Naiba Mountains. They are prominent in many prophecies and are highly blessed."

Tom said, "This country is indeed beautiful and, except for some elvish singing, seems completely unoccupied."

Cearl laughed and said, "You have yet to learn how to perceive the presence of elves. My people dwell in such harmony with nature in these blessed lands that they seem to blend into the landscape."

By late afternoon, they left the mountains and descended into an old forest. The dying sun penetrated the forest floor in beams of light and beneath their feet they walked on a soft cushion of needles. The breeze made a soft rustling sound that gently rocked the treetops. They left the elf roads and paths in the mountains but they still followed the path shown to Tom in the glow of the stone. Tom noticed that Etain seemed agitated once they entered the forest. She began to fly off in different directions and reappeared from others.

"What is Etain doing?" Tom asked Cearl.

"We are now beyond the blessed lands so she scouts our perimeter to report any danger," replied Cearl.

As the day drew to an end, they entered a small meadow in the forest and decided to rest for the night. They started to unpack when Lord Ceowulf announced, "I have no need for rest. I shall continue and send word to you from Etain."

"No!" shouted Willet, "We shall remain together!"

Willet dropped his pack, grabbed his staff and faced Lord Ceowulf.

"My heart burns and I will not rest as long as the stone is lost," said Lord Ceowulf.

"I can not bear to think of one of the sacred stones being desecrated by a foul and evil creature such as the troll who now has it."

"I share your concern, Lord Ceowulf, but I must tell you that something strange happened when we found this troll. The stone glowed brightly as the one that Master Tom wears. I do not pretend to understand this but it should be looked into carefully. I believe we must recover both the stone and the troll."

Lord Ceowulf grabbed the hilt of his sword and shouted, "No! I will not listen to such talk! The sacred stones must remain in the possession of the elf lords until the sons of light are revealed!"

Willet gripped his staff tightly and pointed it towards Lord Ceowulf's face saying, "Beware, lest your presumptions and desire to bear one of the sacred stones lead to your ruin!"

Lord Ceowulf stared defiantly at Willet while his fingers fidgeted with the hilt of his sword. Slowly, Lord Ceowulf's face softened and he relaxed.

"I do not deny that I have longed to possess one of the sacred stones. Now that Lord Swefred is gone, I am next in rank to assume this honor. You can not deny that it is my right to take it!"

Willet replied, "By tradition you are right. However, there is a mystery at work that requires caution, and not bold actions and assumptions."

"I fear that your judgment is wrong," replied Lord Ceowulf.

"I believe this troll is like all his kind. He will not seek us out and will either keep the stone or deliver it to even greater evil.

"However, if by some miracle, the troll returns the stone and cooperates, I agree not to harm him."

"Swear that you will not break this fellowship until we have recovered the stone," said Willet.

"So be it!" said Lord Ceowulf sourly as he turned away to unpack.

Tom was amazed at how quickly the dispute and the tension that it caused dissipated. Lord Ceowulf methodically unpacked and lay down as if to sleep. Tom noted that his eyes remained open and asked Willet, "Does Lord Ceowulf sleep?"

Willet replied, "He travels in spirit but I doubt he will find what he seeks."

Tom asked, "Do we travel in spirit this night?"

Willet replied, "No, it is too dangerous. Look to the horizon. See the flashes of light? There is another convergence of spirits over the portal we passed last night."

Tom wrapped himself in a blanket, laid down on the pine needles, and was soon sound asleep.

In his dreams, Tom saw the image of his father passing from tree to tree at the edge of the clearing near their camp.

"Father! Father! Over here! It's Tom!" he yelled and ran to him.

At first his father continued to wander as if in a daze, but when Tom approached, he stopped and looked at him. He seemed to be only half awake as he asked, "Tom? My son? Is that you?"

"Yes father! It's me! I have missed you!" he said as he gave his father a hug.

"Tom, Tom," his father replied and started to weep. "How I wish this was not just a dream and that you would return home. I miss you terribly!"

Tom started to weep also and said, "This is more than a dream! I am really here! Look at the company sleeping by the campfire. You will find me lying there!"

His father just stared vacantly in the direction Tom indicated and said, "I see nothing Tom. It is good to see you, even if it is just a dream."

"Your father's spirit is more alert than most but he will not remember much when this dream ends," said Willet, who had suddenly appeared next to Tom.

"When men who have not been born into this world dream, their spirits wander in this world in a semi-conscious state and they have few or confused memories of their visit."

As Willet talked to Tom, his father resumed his aimless wandering through the forest. Tom started after him but Willet wrapped his arm around his shoulders and said, "Let him be. There is nothing you can do for him now. Behold! The twilight in the eastern sky announces the dawn, and your father's spirit must soon return to the portal."

Tom wept as he watched his father's spirit disappear into the forest and whispered, "Forgive me, father, for leaving you. I shall come to you. I pray that you will remember this meeting and know that I am well."

Willet comforted him and said, "I believe this meeting

was more than coincidence. After the stone is recovered, I shall help you with your wish."

The next morning they continued through the forest, following the path from the glow of the stone. By mid-day they reached two small alpine lakes that Tom recognized from passing over them two nights ago. Etain continued to appear and disappear into the surrounding forest, returning to either Willet or Lord Ceowulf with scouting reports.

By mid-afternoon Tom noticed that Etain had been gone for an unusually long time and asked Willet, "What happened to Etain?"

Willet replied, "Lord Ceowulf sent her to Prince Caelin to see if he has found the troll and to tell him our position and heading. Lord Ceowulf has scouted this ground in spirit last night and found no danger. This has been confirmed by Etain throughout the day so it is unlikely we will encounter any danger while she is gone."

THE AMBUSH

"GET UP YOU SLUGGARDS!" AMHAS yelled as he kicked the nearest sleeping troll.

"We have work to do if we are going to catch some fish today!"

Amhas was the master of a rogue band of trolls who had formerly served Devlin. He had led them through several battles with elves before he decided that wars were short on plunder and long on risk. He had persuaded them to desert Devlin and for the past three years they wandered from place to place preying on unsuspecting travelers. They had arrived at this site the previous day and found a cave in which to spend the night. The cave was near a pass through a ridge of boulders, which made it a good hideout.

With the dawn they unpacked a large net, which they hauled to the pass and buried. Four trolls hid among the rocks, each with a thick vine tied to a corner of the net. Amhas and another troll grabbed clubs and also hid nearby. Their job was to club to death anyone that they captured. Amhas figured this would be a good location since he knew there had been a battle in the area. There would likely be groups of fugitives, messengers and warriors carrying plunder moving through this pass.

It was mid-afternoon when Min approached a ridge of boulders that stretched as far as he could see. The path shown by the stone required him to climb over and around boulders rather than taking what appeared to be a pass visible in the distance.

Min felt uneasy and shook his head as he said to the stone, "I sure hope you know what you're doing. This doesn't seem to be the most direct and easiest way to me." The light from the stone did not waver or change so Min sighed and began to climb.

His concern grew when he reached the summit of the ridge and the path continued along the top instead of going down the other side. Min soon came to a cave in the rocks overlooking a pass below. A smoldering fire and scattered items of food and clothing told him that trolls had recently been inside. Sensing danger, he crawled to the edge of a rock ledge at the mouth of the cave and looked down at the pass below. Only ten feet below him was a troll hiding behind a boulder and holding a thick rope.

Like Min, he was staring intently at the pass below but he did not notice Min who was above and behind him. Although he could not see his face, the troll below him was deformed and reeked of evil. Min recoiled in shock and rolled onto his back, trying to remain silent while his heart pounded and he gasped for air.

"I have never seen such a foul looking troll! How could this be?" he asked himself.

As if in answer, he felt the weight of the stone and looking down noticed it was glowing brighter. Placing the stone inside his shirt, he crept back to the ledge and again looked down. The troll below had not moved but he looked quite ordinary and much less threatening. Pulling the stone out of his shirt restored the previous hideous vision. Min contemplated the meaning of what he had seen for several minutes until a familiar glow caught his attention.

Entering the pass below was a small group of men and elves led by a wizard and a young lad with a similar glowing stone around his neck. Min immediately recognized them from their resemblance to the spirits he had seen in his vision. He felt a strange bond of fellowship with the lad and others below while he had a sense of revulsion for the troll. As he watched them enter the pass, a surge of fear gripped him as he realized he was about to witness an ambush!

"What should I do?" he asked himself.

"I can not betray my kinsfolk, but I must warn those in the pass below."

Precious minutes passed as he struggled with his thoughts until a horn blast announced the start of the attack. Min saw the troll beneath him begin to pull rapidly on the rope and then the group in the pass was engulfed in a huge net and cloud of dust. Two evil looking trolls with clubs emerged from behind the rocks and hurried toward their netted prey.

Min's heart burned within him and he felt a flow of energy enter his body from the glowing stone. Lifting a large rock with both hands he jumped off the ledge and onto the troll below, striking him on the head with the stone. The net immediately became unbalanced and spilled the group onto the ground just as the two trolls converged on them. Three other trolls appeared and also descended on the mayhem below.

Although he was frightened, he acted without further hesitation because he was driven by concern for the victims in the net.

"I must help them!" he told himself as he grabbed a club beside the fallen troll. He jumped into the pass behind one of the trolls that had been pulling the rope on the opposite side of the pass. With one swing of his club, he dispatched the troll from behind and continued to run towards the center of the fight.

Amhas found himself engaged in combat with an elf lord while the rest of the "fish" in his net had escaped and were fighting the three trolls converging on the net from the opposite end of the pass. He knew that his best chance was to hem the elf lord against the rocky side of the pass where he could nullify the mobility advantage of the elf.

As Amhas and the elf lord exchanged blows, he began to wonder where the two sluggards on his side of the net had gone. Although he had been cut several times, he managed to keep close to the elf lord and drove him into a cleft in the ravine wall. When the elf lord stumbled backwards on a protruding rock shelf, Amhas sensed his chance to deal a killing blow. As he raised his arm to deliver it, he suddenly was pushed forward and into the rock wall next to the elf lord. The blow lifted him off his feet and threw him head first into the rock wall, knocking him unconscious.

One moment Lord Ceowulf was preparing to parry a serious blow from the troll and the next he found himself facing something different all together. He stared dumb founded at another troll that had apparently pushed his adversary into the rock wall! He could not believe that this troll had just harmed one of his kinsfolk to save him! Then his eyes fell on the glowing stone around the troll's neck and Lord Ceowulf was filled with indignation and rage.

"Give up the stone, spawn of Devlin!" he shouted and raised his sword to Min's throat.

Min instinctively backed away from the elf lord, afraid and confused as to why he was being threatened. Lord Ceowulf advanced with his sword to Min's throat driving him backwards across the pass to the opposite wall. With a menacing grin, Lord Ceowulf repeated his command, "Give me the stone and I will spare your life!"

Before Min could reply, an explosion of light temporarily blinded him. When he recovered, he saw that the old man in his vision had driven the blade away and was standing between the elf lord and himself.

"Leave him be!" shouted Willet.

"You shall not harm him!"

CONFRONTATION

*T*HEY WERE SUDDENLY LIFTED UP into the air and then dumped onto the ground. Tom and the others instinctively untangled and found themselves dodging, running and otherwise avoiding several attacking trolls. Fortunately, they were not very agile. However, the small confines of the ravine made it challenging to avoid them.

Cearl, Wini, and Willet were constantly looking after Tom, shouting warnings and instructions and diverting the attention of the trolls. Fortunately, the skirmish did not last long. Once they escaped the net the advantage of surprise was gone. A brief but intense fight followed, which ended soon after Cearl shot the largest troll in the eye with an arrow. Once he fell, the remaining two trolls fled into the surrounding rocks as quickly as they had appeared.

Min knelt down and dropped his club in awe and wonder.

Even though he was looking at the back of the wizard he was struck by the power of his presence.

"You shall not harm him!" Willet repeated as he faced Lord Ceowulf.

"This is an abomination!" replied Lord Ceowulf. "By all that we hold sacred, the stone must be given to me!"

"Behold! See how the stone glows!" shouted Willet. "There must be a purpose to this that we must seek to understand!"

The others gathered around as Willet and Lord Ceowulf argued. Lord Ceowulf appealed to Cearl and Penda, but they stood by Willet, Tom, and Wini.

Seeing that he was alone, he backed away from Willet and said, "It seems that at the moment you have the advantage, but I warn you that there are many elves that will see this my way and will follow me! I will not rest until I have the stone!"

He continued backing away until he reached the rocks behind him, and then disappeared with lightening speed.

Turning towards Min, Willet said, "Please excuse Lord Ceowulf; he, unlike us, does not appreciate what you have done."

Willet bowed and then pointed towards the sprawled body of Amhas, "Thank you for your help. You are most welcome to join our company. We offer you our friendship."

Min smiled and said, "Friends? Yes, please! I would like to know what it is like to have friends!"

Willet looked at the others, who nodded affirmatively. He said to Min, "A friend you have proven to be and shall remain as long as you are true to us."

Willet smiled but then became serious and said, "We can not return to the elves. I fear what Lord Ceowulf said is true.

We must go into hiding until the mysterious actions of the stone in the possession of this troll are understood."

Willet led them into the nearby cave to think and regroup. Amhas regained consciousness in time to hear Willet speak of the seeing stone. He had pretended to be dead until they left and then he followed them to the mouth of the cave.

Once inside, Willet said, "We must flee this place at once, for there will soon be many seeking us. We will go to a secret place called Hadrian's Keep."

Reaching into his robe, he pulled out a flask and poured its contents into a depression on the cave floor, forming a puddle three feet across. As soon as the liquid hit the floor it started to bubble as though boiling.

Willet closed his eyes and whispered something that was unintelligible to Tom.

Willet opened his eyes and said, "Quickly, everyone must step in before it is gone! Tom, you first!"

Tom stepped in and seemed to sink into the floor of the cave. One by one they followed. Willet was last and joined them as the last of the liquid vaporized off the floor of the cave leaving no trace of their passage.

"Hadrian's Keep!" whispered Amhas.

"I have never heard of it but I know someone who will pay handsomely for information leading to two seeing stones!"

HADRIAN'S KEEP

$\mathcal{T}$OM FOUND HIMSELF STANDING ON a narrow ledge next to a sheer rock wall at least one hundred feet high. As the others appeared, he noticed that they were about half way up the side of a steep, wooded ravine. The rumble of cascading water down in the ravine told him there must be a stream obscured by the trees below.

"Come along!" said Willet as he took the lead. "We still have some distance to cover and the day is nearly spent."

There was no path to follow but Willet seemed to know the way. They followed the rock wall climbing over boulders; through tickets of brush and soon were inside a dense forest.

"At least we are going down hill," Tom thought as he walked behind Min.

The ground descended into the ravine and gradually the roar of flowing water faded. When they finally reached the bottom, the ravine had narrowed until they were walking on a rocky streambed. Eventually, the ravine became so narrow that it was nearly dark at the bottom and Min had to occasionally turn sideways to pass through.

Although it was only late afternoon, it soon became completely dark and they had to feel their way along the walls. They seemed to make a sharp bend and then there was faint light ahead indicating the end of the narrows. When they reached the source of the light, the ravine walls suddenly expanded to reveal a broad meadow a mile wide surrounded by three mountains.

The stream emerged from the base of the mountain to their left. Ahead of them was an alpine meadow in which there were white, yellow, purple, and orange flowers. The mountains were capped with snow, which glistened on the west facing peaks in the late afternoon sun. Evergreen trees formed a dark canopy on the slopes except for where there were patches of barren rocks of many sizes and shapes. The middle mountain had only scattered trees that seemed to grow from a rocky forest of boulders and spires.

"That is our destination," announced Willet as he pointed to the group of boulders and spires jutting out of the side of the middle mountain.

"Behold, Hadrian's Keep!"

Tom replied, "I see nothing but some barren rocks strewn about the mountain side."

"Precisely!" said Willet. "The dwarves built this fortress using the natural rock features. At this distance, it is virtually invisible to the untrained eye."

The first of the evening stars had just appeared when they rounded a large rock pinnacle at the base of the middle mountain and saw an arched tunnel twenty feet high.

"We camp here tonight," said Willet.

"This is the main entrance to the Keep."

"If this is a fortress, where is everyone?" asked Wini.

"Excellent question Master Wini!" said Willet as he began to unpack. "The answer requires some explanation, which I will gladly give once we have unpacked and eaten."

Cearl and Penda shot a few rabbits, which made an excellent stew when mixed with some buntatas and carrots that Princess Linette had sent along. Min was very attentive to everyone's needs and tried hard to be liked and accepted. He was particularly drawn to Tom. He sensed a deep but unknown bond that somehow tied them to the power of the stones they carried.

Wini complained about Min's behavior and whined, "Stop doting on me like an over-sized sheep dog! I can do it myself! I am not used to having a servant look to my needs!"

It was dark by the time they finished eating, so they unrolled their blankets near the campfire and gathered around it. As the darkness grew deeper they lay on their blankets and watched the fire change from yellow flames to crackling red embers. Tom's eyelids began to feel heavy when Min grabbed some wood next to him and threw it onto the fire. This seemed to rouse Wini who said, "Please, Master Willet, tell us about this place."

Willet stretched and yawned. He wrapped his blanket around himself said, "Very well. However, this tale will take some time to tell."

He looked around and, after seeing that they had roused themselves to listen, began by saying, "Long ago in the early days of the first age of the earth, the race of dwarves originated in these mountains. Legend has it that they were the result of the union of humans who mined these mountains and elves in the surrounding woodlands.

In those days, the Titans spawned by Devlin's demons were exterminating the human race. Soon, humans became scarce and widely scattered. Only in a few remote areas, such as these mountains, were there any numbers left. In those days the elves gathered from throughout the earth to challenge the Titans and save the remnants of the human race.

There was a fierce battle between the elves and the Titans in the Forest of Mordula on the opposite side of these mountains. The battle raged for several weeks with tremendous losses on both sides, and ended in a stalemate. The remnants of both armies scattered and a few elves retreated into the mountains and lived with the humans. These elves and men lived together for many years until the Creator removed the humans. During this time, the race of dwarves is said to have originated from the union of elves and men.

After the humans were taken away by the Creator, the elves departed and the dwarves retreated deep into the mountains and remained hidden. They dug deep into the mountains and developed underground cities. After the passing of many generations, they emerged on the backside of the mountains in a secret place where they built this keep you see around you in honor of King Hadrian.

King Hadrian was the wisest and most powerful of all the dwarf rulers. He forged new alliances with the elves while keeping the location of this place a secret. He was interested in studying history and magic, so he sent scribes to various places to find or copy books about the ancient ways.

The dwarves were masters at secrecy and kept all of the entrances into these mountains well hidden. Few were allowed to visit and those who did had to be blindfolded. This keep was built in such an inaccessible place and in such a way that it would be invisible at a distance. Even within this keep, its passages and dwellings are so well blended into the mountain that they can not be found without a guide or secret knowledge that the dwarves kept to themselves.

Inside this keep is a vast library that contains knowledge of deep magic and wisdom matched only by the libraries of Princess Linette and Andhun. However, even they do not know of its existence.

"How, then, did you find this place?" asked Cearl.

"Find?" laughed Willet. "No, dear Cearl, you give me too much credit! I did not find this place. However, your question is timely and leads me to another story.

As a wizard of the Order of Alastrine, one of my duties was to study and preserve ancient knowledge. Consequently, I spent considerable time in the storage vaults of Princess Linette's library in Taliesin reading ancient scrolls and texts that were rarely used. During one of these searches, I came across a scroll that recorded the visits of dwarves to Taliesin. My curiosity was aroused as I had never met a dwarf and knew little of them. I continued to search for more information and came across several books that described their origins, customs, and lineage. I was intrigued by their curious blend of elfish and human traits. I decided to pursue my new interest by visiting the homeland of the dwarves in the Forbidden Mountains.

Although the distance was great and required many months of travel by land and sea, my journey passed uneventfully. Eventually, I reached the Forest of Mordula that borders these mountains. The forest had long since recovered from the battle and there was no evidence of its occurrence.

I spent several days wandering the Forbidden Mountains in search of an entrance or the presence of dwarves but found neither. I decided that if there were any dwarves, they were probably deep within the mountains and would not be found without more time and effort than I was prepared to spend. I decided to return to Taliesin and was descending the mountains when I came across a small alpine lake nestled in a wooded valley.

I descended to the lake and was enjoying an invigorating swim when I noticed something unnatural. While there were birds singing and other forest animals where I was, across the lake there were none. I followed the shore and, as I approached the area, there was an unnatural silence. My heart began to pound as I sensed a close but undefined danger.

I heard a faint moaning, which I followed until I came to a small clearing in the forest. In the center of the clearing was a small man about half the height of an adult human. He was very hairy with a curly, red beard and frizzy hair. He seemed to be in a trance and stared blankly into space moving only slightly to emit a sorrowful moan. From the waist down where his legs should have been, there was the trunk of a tree. As I watched, I could see that he was slowly being transformed by a spell. Fortunately, the spell was within my knowledge and power and I was able to reverse it.

I gathered some herbs and made him a potion that accelerated his recovery. After sleeping for a day, he awoke and told me his name was Behlin. He was a scribe who had set out from the dwarves' City of Moganda, which was located inside one of the nearby mountains. Some gnomes had ambushed him, took his possessions, and cast a spell upon him. When I told him of my interest in dwarves he agreed to take me to his people, but I had to be blindfolded. I agreed and was taken deep into the mountains where I remained with the dwarves for several years.

I came to know a considerable amount of their language and customs but much less of the maze of tunnels, halls, and dwellings under those mountains. I was taken to the far side of the mountains to the library located in Hadrian's Keep. Behlin told me that the mountains were very rugged and quite impassible from the surface. When I commented on the length of our journey to the far side, he said that the Forbidden Mountains were a hundred miles wide and three times as long as the crow flies.

I was treated with dignity and found the dwarves to be quite friendly despite the fact that I was never allowed to go anywhere unescorted. Behlin and I became good friends and learned much from each other. I even had the honor of meeting King Raegenheri, who was the great grandson of King Hadrian.

My studies progressed quite well. I even gained weight having become fond of dwarfish cooking, which was heavy on meats, buntatas, mushrooms, and spices. In the center of the library at Hadrian's Keep, there was a large, white rock fifteen feet high that jutted out of the smooth and polished floor. It was unlike the surrounding stone makeup of the mountain and its origin was unknown. Some said that it was the remains of a meteor that fell from the sky and buried itself in the mountain.

During the day, beams of sunlight fell on this rock from a

skylight in the mountainside. The light beams were reflected about the room in an ever-changing kaleidoscope of white patches of light. At night, the stone glowed with a faint green luminescence. As wondrous as these things were, the most intriguing aspect of this rock was the strange inscriptions carved from floor to ceiling on its eastern side. This tablet was inscribed with words from an ancient tongue that defied translation despite the efforts of many generations of learned and dedicated scribes. The dwarves considered this place sacred and their veneration of it inspired them to develop the vast library that surrounds it.

One day a disturbance arose among the dwarf leaders. It seems that, during my stay, one of their prominent scribes named Miran returned from the library of Andhun with a copy of *The Once and Forever Ruler.* Every time this book was opened, some form of enchantment must have been at work since most of those who read from it became followers of the beliefs in it. Only a few who read it refused to accept its teachings. Many more believed it was a false book because it contradicted the teachings of *The Past and Future King.*

I tried to persuade Miran and his followers that they were being misled, but they would not listen. The visions and deceptive magic of Devlin were at work in those who read *The Once and Forever Ruler.* Soon the followers of Miran grew proud and considered themselves far more enlightened than those who refused to believe. They looked at those who held to traditional beliefs as closed minded and ignorant.

Most dwarves know little of magic except for the few scribes who studied the ancient texts. However, even ordinary dwarves who read *The Once And Forever Ruler* began to perform magical feats that seemed to confirm the authenticity of the book.

At first, these magical feats were mostly of the mischievous sort as the followers of Miran taunted the others by playing tricks on them. However, the animosity between the two groups continued to grow and the magic became malicious. The controversy became so intense that it split families and threatened to destroy them. King Raegenheri became alarmed and decided to banish the followers of Miran. He permanently closed all the entrances to the mountains so they could not return.

Those who were banished scattered and lived in small wandering groups like gypsies. Consistent with their kin they preferred to remain separate and secretive. They continued to practice their mischievous magic on whoever crossed their path. However, they particularly disliked their brother dwarves for rejecting them and swore to punish any that they found. In order to distinguish themselves from the other dwarves, they called themselves gnomes and developed their own dress and customs.

I, too, was politely but firmly escorted out when the gnomes were banished. King Raegenheri proclaimed that his people were to return to the deep places in the mountains so I returned to Taliesin. Rather than destroy Hadrian's Keep, King Raegenheri ordered the destruction of its passages into the mountains. Before doing so, the scribes copied essential books such as *The Past and Future King* and took them deep into the mountains. They left the library intact and under the care of some scribes, including Behlin, who volunteered to continue their studies.

Willet paused and then said, "It has been hundreds of

years since I parted company with Behlin. By the life span of dwarves, it is unlikely that he is still alive. Nevertheless, I hope that he or some other scribe remains and can guide us to the sacred stone in the library."

"What happens if none remain?" asked Tom.

"Then I will do my best, but I fear our progress will be slow as I am little better than a blind man when it comes to deciphering the maze of passages within this Keep," replied Willet.

"Now it is time to rest. I have talked away more of the night than I had intended."

THE WALSTRUM

A COLD AND DAMP MIST WOKE Tom from a deep sleep. It was still dark and fog had settled into the valley, reducing visibility to almost nothing. Tom could make out the forms of everyone in their party except for Willet, who was not where Tom had last seen him. Willet, like the elves, did not sleep as men do but remained stationary with open eyes. Sensing alarm, Tom nudged Cearl and Wini, who were lying next to him.

"Willet is missing," Tom whispered.

"I'll find him," Cearl replied and quickly vanished into the fog.

After a few tense moments, Cearl reappeared and said, "He comes."

Tom and Wini stared at the place indicated by Cearl but saw nothing but a gray wall of mist. Slowly, the silhouette of Willet appeared but he was not alone. Next to him was a short, stout man about half of Willet's height. They stopped and were conversing in low voices just far enough away that

Tom could not clearly see or hear them. The short man nodded his head and disappeared into the mist.

Willet approached and said briskly, "Wake up! We must pack and leave at once!"

Instead of entering the tunnel, Willet led them through the fog in what seemed to be aimless wandering to Tom. They traveled in single file with Willet in the lead followed by Tom, Cearl, Wini, Min, and Penda. The fog thickened and, although he was only a few paces ahead, Tom could barely see Willet's back.

"It seems like we are walking in circles. Why didn't we enter through the tunnel?" Tom asked Willet.

"The tunnel entrance is closed," replied Willet. "We are almost there."

They entered a narrow cleft in the rocks, which sloped steeply downwards. They had to concentrate on their footing and wedge themselves in the rocks or hold onto the walls to keep from sliding. Soon they descended into darkness and proceeded slowly by feeling the walls and floor. Tom looked back and saw that the entrance above them had shrunk to a small grey slit. Fear began to well up inside him and he was about to question Willet when he noticed that the slope abruptly leveled off and they found themselves standing on a slab of rock inside of a cave.

Willet shouted, "Tanaufel heulo!"

A ball of blue light appeared above Willet's head that was so bright that Tom could not look directly at it.

"This way! We are not far from the entrance," said Willet.

Willet led them through a narrow winding tunnel that ended in a precipitous drop into blackness. As they gathered on the ledge, Tom looked across the chasm and saw a small man standing about fifty feet away on a ledge along the opposite wall.

"Wes ou hal! Welcome!" shouted the small man who picked up a large stone wrapped in many interwoven vines and threw it across to Willet. After he removed the stone, Willet unwrapped the thick vines to reveal a rope bridge. Willet attached the ends of the bridge to four metal rings in the rock wall. Once they were all across, the little man gave three quick pulls on each of the four rope supports and they all came loose.

"How did he do that?" asked Wini.

"Dwarf slip knots," replied Willet. "It's one of the skills you learn while living with them."

"Greetings! Dehlin, son of Behlin!" said Willet as he bowed to the little man.

Dehlin returned the bow and then finished repacking the rope bridge. Dehlin was stocky but muscular. He had long, curly, red hair and a long, frizzy beard just as Willet had described Behlin. However, Dehlin was dressed in chain mail to his knees and wore a helmet with a long bridge that extended over his nose. On his back he had a long, leather sheath that held a double-edged axe. Over one shoulder was a leather strap attached to a pouch that rested on his side. A cross bow and arrows were visible inside the pouch.

Dehlin embraced each of them in turn and said, "Welcome, Willet, master wizard! I am honored to have you stay with us again!"

"Welcome elves! It has been too long since any of your kin have dwelled in this mountain!"

"Welcome son of light! Your presence gives me renewed faith and hope in the ancient prophecies!"

When he came to Min, he paused awkwardly and did not know what to say. Min shuffled his feet nervously and hung his head as if embarrassed by who he was.

After thinking a moment longer, Dehlin said, "I never thought I would see the day when a troll befriended elves and humans. You must be quite an exceptional fellow to have won the friendship of such a distinguished group!"

Min's face brightened into a sheepish grin and he picked Dehlin up off the floor and gave him a bear hug that buried the dwarf within Min's massive arms. After Dehlin mumbled something about suffocating, Min set him down.

He greeted Wini and said to everyone, "Follow me!"

"My father is anxious to meet you. His time to pass is near, yet he lingers by the strength of his will. He has foreseen your arrival and believes that he will not die until he sees you."

Dehlin led them through a labyrinth of tunnels, halls and rooms of various sorts. They did not see any other dwarves or signs of life. The rooms and halls were well furnished and in order, but the covers on the furniture and the coating of dust bore witness to the many years since the dwarves had left the Keep.

Tom asked Dehlin, "Are you and Behlin alone? It looks like nobody has been here for many years."

Dehlin replied, "There are few of us who guard this place and fewer who study the ancient books. Fifty is our number, of which a dozen are scribes like my father, while the rest of us are warriors who keep this place a secret. There are no women or children, as we have set aside these pleasures and responsibilities to focus on our dedication to this sacred place.

Soon you will see the others, as we have gathered to honor my father in his last days."

As they walked through the Keep, Tom would occasionally stop and look out of one of the many windows cut into the side of the mountain. The views were a spectacular and mesmerizing combination of jutting rocks and sheer cliffs overlooking the lush, green meadow and the stream that they had crossed the previous day. Tom could see that the Keep was well hidden and there was only one approach, which could be observed and protected from many places.

They continued to walk up, down, through, and around many hallways and rooms until Tom was thoroughly confused. He began to think that Dehlin was purposely trying to confuse them by taking far less than a direct route. Eventually, they arrived at two massive wooden doors in a carved stone arch. The doors had rows of intricate wooden panels depicting the line of dwarf kings.

Dehlin motioned for them to gather around and said, "Wait here until I return. The Walstrum for my father has begun."

Dehlin quietly opened one of the large doors just enough to enter and quickly closed it again. Tom caught a glimpse of a vast room and could hear music and singing.

After Dehlin closed the door, Tom asked, "What is a Walstrum?"

Willet replied, "It is the formal rite of passage for dwarves who are near death. There are songs of honor, stories of past times enjoyed together, and the presentation of gifts and blessings for each dwarf that is present. It is the celebration of the good that Behlin has brought to others. Dehlin, as his son, will go last and then we will be admitted."

Willet explained the history of the dwarf kings depicted on the door panels. They waited for several hours before the doors slowly opened and Dehlin motioned for them to come in.

"My father will see you now."

The large doors swung slowly open to reveal a cavernous room filled with furniture, rugs, tapestries, paintings, statues, and enormous bookshelves. There were several galleries containing books visible in the rock walls above the floor.

Tom estimated that the ceiling must have been over one hundred feet high. In the center of the open space directly ahead was a semicircle of chairs in which fifty dwarves were seated. In the center was a very old dwarf reclining on a couch, which was on a stage with three steps. A large luminescent rock emerged from the floor behind the stage. It was this glowing rock that drew and captivated the gaze of each member of the group as they entered the room. They stood transfixed and stared in awe at the large rock, which pulsated with energy.

Willet was the first to recover and began to recite praises for Behlin in a poetic manner as he advanced towards him. The musicians accompanied Willet in the fashion of the Walstrum ceremony. As if on cue, all of the dwarves rose and faced them as Tom and the others fell in behind Willet. Tom felt a burning sensation on his chest and pulled out the seeing stone, which glowed brightly. Turning around, he noticed that Min also had exposed his seeing stone, which glowed so brightly that it left a spot in Tom's vision when he looked away.

They stopped at the bottom of the platform on which Behlin was feebly standing by leaning upon his staff. The music suddenly stopped and, after exchanging bows with Willet, Behlin said, "Although I am at death's door, my heart leaps for joy at the sight before me. The Creator is kind and faithful in allowing me to see you again, dear Willet, my old friend."

"It is our privilege to honor such a wise and great teacher as yourself. Our loss will be severe but your gain once your spirit passes through death will be fantastic!"

At Willet's words, a slight smile passed across Behlin's face and he nodded his head in agreement. Tom sensed that Behlin eagerly anticipated the end of this life and the beginning of a new and better one. Though Behlin was feeble and aged, Tom sensed power and vigor deep within him.

Tom thought to himself, "He is at peace and is ready for the next life. He reminds me of a caterpillar about to transform into a butterfly."

Behlin raised his voice so all could hear and said, "Long have I hoped for this day! As my kinsmen can attest, I received a vision now almost one hundred years ago in which I was told that I would not see death until my eyes beheld the first of the sons of light."

"Aye! It is so!" shouted the dwarves in unison.

Behlin continued, "On this day the promise made to me has been fulfilled! Behold! See how the glowing stones confirm the Creator's presence and the display of His will!"

Behlin turned towards Dehlin and the dwarves and said, "Brothers, my final wish is that you swear to protect and serve the sons of light and this sacred place. What say you?"

Dehlin and the dwarves answered, "Aye! We so swear!"

Behlin raised his arms with palms upturned and said, "Now comes the changing of days when a child shall arise and lead the faithful. Now dawns the time when the present order will be remade!"

He looked at Min and his face beamed with joy as he said, "Who could have predicted that a troll would be among the sons of light! How wondrous are the ways of the Creator, for they are beyond our understanding or prediction!"

Behlin closed his eyes and began a dwarf song of praise and worship to the Creator. One by one Willet and the dwarves joined in. Tom longed to join them but he had never heard this song and so he felt left out.

As Tom listened, he closed his eyes and began to hum the melody of the song. The stone around his neck felt warm and Tom sensed that energy was building within it. He realized that the stone was responding to the song of worship to the Creator. The desire and frustration at not being able to sing increased within him until he asked the Creator to help him. As if in response, Tom felt a surge of energy from deep inside that seemed to well up within him until it reached his mouth. He began to sing with Willet and the dwarves as though he were a dwarf!

Tom felt intense excitement and joy similar to what he experienced at the bridge to Taliesin. As Tom sang, he felt a tingling sensation in his hand. When he looked at it, he was surprised to see that it glowed with the same bright light that came from the stone! The glow spread throughout his body until he felt like he was about to burst with energy.

Suddenly, a light beam shot from his seeing stone and directed itself to Behlin who started to glow like Tom. One by one, the light spread throughout the room, filling and connecting them all while they sang more enthusiastically. Tom felt the urge to move over to the large rock. As he did so, he noticed that the others were joining him and forming a circle around it.

Tom had never before known such rapture and joy. He felt an intense closeness and unity with the Creator and the others. The sacred rock began to glow and vibrate with increasing intensity until the surrounding mountain shook. As their singing reached a crescendo, a burst of light as bright as the sun exploded from the sacred rock and blinded them so that they covered their eyes and fell to the ground. Their singing ended abruptly and they lay upon the floor as though they were dead.

Tom remained face down on the floor for several minutes with his eyes closed. He continued to praise and worship the Creator mentally as he dwelled on the awesome events he had just experienced. Deep within his being he felt great joy and peace. This was like waking from the best dream he ever had. Slowly, he became aware of the coolness of the smooth rock floor. He opened his eyes and gazed at the stone on his chest. It was glowing faintly as though spent from the previous display of energy. He looked next to him and found himself face to face with Behlin. His face was radiant which aroused more emotion from Tom.

"I have never seen anyone happier than Behlin," he said to himself.

As Tom continued to look at Behlin, he realized that his eyes were not blinking. In fact, he was not moving or breathing at all!

Tom jumped up from the floor and shouted, "Arise! Behlin is dead!"

The others began to move as if they were waking from a deep sleep. They gathered around Behlin's body but none dared to touch him. There was no sorrow or mourning for all who looked upon him could see that he had passed with great honor and now was enthralled to be with his Creator.

As Tom looked at Behlin, he wished that he, too, could some day die like this. Tom moved his gaze from the old dwarf's face and noticed that one of his arms was outstretched and his hand was pointing towards the sacred rock. When he looked at the rock, he was awestruck and dropped to his knees staring at the carved stone tablet. When the others saw Tom, they looked at the stone tablet and likewise knelt in reverent awe.

"The words! I can read the words!" Tom whispered.

The words chiseled into the stone tablet that had previously been incomprehensible had been reformed and were legible! Slowly and thoughtfully, they began to read the words, which said:

> *I will destroy the wisdom of the wise*
> *The intelligence of the intelligent I will frustrate.*
> *For my ways are not your ways*
> *Nor are my thoughts your thoughts.*
> *Great and marvelous are my ways*
> *For as high as the heavens are above*
> *the earth*
> *So are my thoughts beyond your*
> *understanding.*

Tom said, "The remaining words are unchanged."

"Indeed, it appears that roughly two-thirds of the words on the tablet still remain as they did before," replied Willet.

"What do you think this means?" asked Tom.

Willet said, "Some things are now apparent but much more remains to be understood. What is obvious is that knowledge and wisdom are revealed by the Creator in the manner and time that suits His purposes."

"Come, let's prepare for Behlin's funeral."

DEVLIN'S REALM

$\mathcal{D}$EEP WITHIN THE EARTH WHERE rock changes to magma, in a place of gloom and deepest night where even the light is like darkness, Devlin sat on his throne surrounded by a vast host of worshipping creatures. There were the spirits of orcs, trolls, werewolves, vampires and other Titans who had died. In addition, the spirits of men who died and had not been born into the first age of the earth resided with Devlin. He noted with pleasure that virtually all of the spirits of mankind were in his presence.

"Everything is proceeding according to my plans," he said to himself.

"The spirits of mankind belong to me! They live their lives in futile pleasures and to the pursuit of trivial things. Their minds are easily deceived and they have been influenced by my demons to suit my purposes!"

These thoughts were interrupted as he shifted his attention to the frenzy of praise and devotion from the ocean of spirits swarming around him. He smiled as he looked about with great satisfaction and pleasure.

He thought to himself, "I am indeed worthy of all praise, honor, and glory! I am most powerful on the earth! The glory and honor given me by this multitude are surely like that of the Creator. Yes, and even greater than the Creator! Their worship is fanatical and without order or restraint. Yes! Powerful it is and ever original in its disorder and chaos to glorify me!"

The vast throng circled around his throne in continuous adoration. He kept most of his demons here to enhance the power and intensity of the worship. Devlin most enjoyed dwelling on thoughts of his greatness and being the focus of such a large and growing swarm. To be worshipped and the focus of continuous adoration was an addictive experience.

The only disturbance that spoiled his revelry was Molech. However, even his visits were less frequent since the deception of Andhun. Devlin congratulated himself on his genius in solving this problem. As powerful and nearly perfect as his spell on humans was, there still were a few that somehow managed to be born into the first age of the earth. Fewer of these survived his assassins soon after their birth. However, with time there came to be a group of humans who managed to survive with the aid of the cursed elves.

Andhun, in particular, was a worrisome threat in that he was given a seeing stone by the elves and appeared to be the first of the sons of light. However, his pride was his downfall and became the means to twist his mind through skillful manipulation so that he became a useful puppet.

Although Andhun and his followers were lost to his realm, they were no longer a threat. Devlin took great pleasure in thinking how he had converted the Creator's children to become his agents, to honor and serve his purposes. He imagined the pain and disappointment that the Creator must feel and this filled him with glee.

His impish delight was abruptly cut short by a disturbance in his worshippers. It was only a small ripple but Devlin immediately recognized it and knew it would grow.

He thought, "I must have had a premonition about Molech, for he is approaching."

The disturbance grew rapidly until even those close to Devlin ceased their worship.

Molech was Devlin's chief general and most dedicated servant. As he approached, the fear that his presence inspired spread among the worshippers. They cowered and then scurried out of the way, resulting in a scene that resembled the parting of the ocean before his advance.

Molech was much larger and more powerful than most of the demons. He, like Devlin, was created as an archangel, which was the highest rank of their kind. Since their rebellion and fall, the demons had retained their ranks.

Whereas Devlin drew pleasure from worship, Molech loved to inspire fear. He had long talons and fangs. His eyes blazed with fire and his wings measured over thirty feet across. Not even Devlin could match his speed of flight. He arrived at the head of one hundred elite demons, called Prygians, who were known for their cruelty.

Molech was obsessed with exerting his power and control over others. He never rested from his efforts to subdue all creatures to the will of Devlin. He rarely went to see Devlin. He preferred to send his subordinates, except when he was summoned, usually for some reason of grave importance. This time he came to Devlin's throne without being summoned and with great haste, which was highly unusual.

Generally, he approached at a much slower pace, which enabled him to enjoy the fear his presence invoked or to kick and abuse some lesser spirits. However, this time he hurried rapidly to the bottom step of Devlin's throne and knelt in submission.

Devlin judged that this visit was of great importance but did not wish to appear greatly concerned. He also enjoyed the display of honor accorded to him by such a distinguished host of his best demons, so he made them hold their submissive pose for longer than customary.

"You may approach and speak," said Devlin to Molech.

"Troublesome events have recently transpired that require your attention," replied Molech.

"Speak!" commanded Devlin.

Molech continued, "Two humans have entered our world and have not been accounted for."

"Not accounted for?" echoed Devlin in a chilling tone that indicated his displeasure.

"Yes, my lord. They escaped our assassins and found refuge among the elves."

Devlin suppressed any sign of concern and said, "What have you done to fix this blunder?"

Molech replied, "An army of orcs under General Crodha was ordered to destroy the elves and the humans."

"And?" replied Devlin, who was becoming impatient to hear the resolution of this matter.

Molech continued, "The attack failed and the orc army was destroyed."

Devlin's anger and alarm continued to rise and he yelled,

"I want General Crodha turned over to my tormentors to pay for his incompetence!"

"General Crodha is dead. I have brought you his spirit," replied Molech sheepishly.

Molech signaled to the demons behind him who dragged a shackled and abused specter of Crodha and threw him at Devlin's feet.

"Speak worm!" commanded Molech.

Groveling and quivering with fear, Crodha spoke in a soft, whimpering voice.

"The attack was proceeding as planned when some elves suddenly appeared behind us and overpowered the trolls. They then turned our catapults against us."

"Enough of your prattling excuses!" Devlin roared. "What of the humans?"

Crodha whimpered, "None were found, but I did find a seeing stone."

Molech grabbed him by the throat and lifted him off of the floor and said, "Why did you not speak of this before? You know I don't like surprises."

Crodha tried to speak but only his lips moved due to Molech's grip on his throat.

"Let him speak," said Devlin.

Desperate to redeem himself, Crodha stood and tried to look proud and said, "I killed Lord Swefred during the battle and took the seeing stone from him."

To kill an elf lord was no small feat. To kill one of great reputation like Lord Swefred and to discover he had one of the twelve seeing stones was either an astonishing revelation or a bold lie. Molech tended to believe the latter was the case. He thought Crodha must have been lying to redeem himself.

"If what you say is true, where is the stone?" asked Molech.

Crodha seemed to shrivel and shrank back onto the floor, "I don't know," he whispered.

"Ha! I thought so!" shouted Molech as he again reached for his throat.

"No! Wait! I can show you where I lost it. It's in the lake near the battle."

"Very well! You shall have a chance to redeem yourself," said Devlin.

Molech said, "The place he speaks of is crawling with elves. We shall have to go in small numbers and in stealth. In case someone has found the stone, the Witch of Ogherune will join us. She can conjure the image of anyone who has taken the stone provided there is a trail to find."

Devlin said, "Do not fail! If we can possess but one of the seeing stones, we can prevent the sons of light from fulfilling the prophecy and defeat the Creator's plans, since He is bound by His words."

"There is more, my lord," said Molech.

"Speak!" commanded Devlin who was both intrigued and impatient.

Molech commanded, "Ragbar, step forward and report!"

One of the demons behind Molech stepped forward and said, "During my watch over Andhun, two humans arrived via the portal in his dining room. One of them was a boy called Tom, son of Throm. This boy carried the very seeing stone that Andhun once possessed. The other was a shepherd named Wini."

"Excellent!" shouted Devlin. "Then we shall soon have his seeing stone. Are these the two humans of which you spoke?"

Molech replied, "They are my lord. However, they escaped through the same portal a short time after their arrival."

A roar like thunder came from Devlin. It was so loud and powerful that it knocked down the demons before him and shook the earth. He strode over to Ragbar and picked him up like a rag doll.

Returning to his throne he opened a large rock slab to one side and threw Ragbar down a shaft shouting after him.

"Your incompetence is hereby rewarded! You are henceforth banished to the lake of fire to be tormented!"

Turning back to Molech he asked, "Anything else?"

Devlin's rage was so intense that even Molech cringed and said, "Recently, there have been two earthquakes that we have not caused and cannot explain."

"Go on!" shouted Devlin who was clearly out of patience.

Molech continued, "One originated among the elf lands near their city of Taliesin and the second was at the opposite end of the earth in the vicinity of the Forbidden Mountains. The intensity in both cases was beyond what would be expected if they were of natural causes."

"Yes, I remember them," replied Devlin. "I thought you had caused them," he said to Molech.

"No, my lord," replied Molech. "Both areas are among those that are closed to demons and other evil spirits, so we have not discovered the causes."

"Then send in werewolves, goblins, gnomes, and the other secretive agents to spy and find out what has happened," commanded Devlin.

Molech bowed and said, "It shall be done, my lord."

Devlin continued, "Find out where this boy, Tom, and this shepherd, Wini, are from. When you do, I want you to assign your best Prygians to attend to their friends and relatives. One of many human weaknesses is their concern for their loved ones. We shall exploit this weakness by using it as a trap to find and destroy them!"

"As you wish, my lord," replied Molech, who bowed and turned to go.

Devlin said, "Wait! I have yet another task for you. I want you to urge Andhun and his followers to accelerate their plans to consolidate power under my influence. Those who will not convert must be destroyed. There must be only one set of universal beliefs among humans as described in *The Once and Forever Ruler!*"

Molech smiled hungrily in anticipation of the fear and destruction that would soon occur as this order was put into effect throughout the earth.

"With pleasure, my lord!" said Molech who again bowed and left at great speed, parting an ocean of spirits before him.

Devlin watched Molech's departure momentarily and thought, "There are plenty of opportunities to thwart the Creator's plans. Even if the two humans turn out to be the first of the sons of light, are there not twelve needed to fulfill the prophecy? As the seeing stones are passed from elves to humans, there should be plenty of opportunities to obtain at least one of them."

After Molech departed, the frenzied worship of Devlin resumed and it captivated his thoughts once more.

LORD CEOWULF'S RETURN

Lord Ceowulf hastened to Taliesin. He went directly to the chamber where the counsel of elf lords was meeting and burst through the doors.

He shouted, "Willet has bewitched the fellowship that set out to recover the seeing stone! The troll keeps the stone and Willet is helping him!"

The council was dumbfounded and several moments of silence ensued while they contemplated this strange news.

Princess Linette was the first to recover and said, "There must be an explanation for Willet's behavior. He has always been true to us and has honored our customs."

Lord Ceowulf interrupted, "I tell you he is a traitor! I'm afraid he has fallen under Devlin's spell and, like Andhun, believes he has some higher knowledge and no longer follows our sacred ways."

Lord Ceowulf then related the events of their journey and meeting with Min.

After he concluded, Princess Linette said, "The fairies shall be sent to the pass you described and to our kin everywhere. We shall not rest until we find them, for grave indeed are the consequences if the seeing stone falls into Devlin's hands."

Turning to Lord Ceowulf, she said, "I think you are too hasty in judging Willet's actions. I will continue to call him elf friend until he proves to be a betrayer."

"Fool!" shouted Lord Ceowulf. "What further proof do you require? His actions have broken faith with our sacred traditions and are clearly those of a traitor!"

Lord Ceowulf instantly regretted his choice of words in addressing Princess Linette, but his pride drove him to continue.

"As elves our duty is to serve the Creator according to the sacred traditions and teachings. We must not waver or compromise the sacred truths that have been bestowed upon us by the Creator. I consider anyone who condones Willet's behavior or compromises our sacred customs to also be a traitor!"

Princess Linette replied, "Then our fellowship is broken! Each must choose the path that seems best suited to the Creator's will."

Lord Ceowulf stormed from the room shouting, "I call upon all elves who desire to preserve the purity of our teachings and hold to them precisely as they have been written to follow me! To Bane-ghial we shall go!"

And thus Lord Ceowulf and one-third of the elves of Taliesin departed to Bane-ghial on the opposite side of the mountain from Taliesin. While there, Lord Ceowulf developed and improved this ancient elf city and searched diligently for the troll with the seeing stone. As word of these events spread, elves from other cities also joined Lord

Ceowulf. They considered themselves to be the guardians of the truth and to be the best among the elves in interpreting and following the ancient teachings of their ancestors.

BEHLIN'S FUNERAL

$\mathcal{B}$EHLIN WAS PLACED IN A glass casket set on a stone table near the sacred rock. His face remained fixed in the expression of joy that marked his death. As was their custom, he was to be buried in the vaults beneath the great library after three days. On the third day the dwarves gathered around the casket and sang a long farewell song. Each dwarf sang solo verses and all joined in the chorus. While they were singing, the large entrance doors slowly swung open and a multitude of voices from outside overwhelmed their chorus.

Turning around, Tom saw a large dwarf dressed in regal robes leading a procession of noble and distinguished looking dwarves. He wore a gold crown and was dressed in burgundy velvet from head to toe. He had short, curly, black hair and a closely-trimmed beard that was an equal mix of white and black hair. Around his waist was a gold belt inlaid with precious stones of various colors. He stared straight ahead and proceeded slowly, holding a gold embossed copy of *The Past and Future King* above his head. The dwarves around

Behlin's casket turned towards the entrance and dropped to one knee, but continued to sing.

"King Raegenheri has returned!" whispered Willet to Tom in answer to his questioning gaze.

"Kneel as the others do to show respect."

The King placed the book he was carrying on the casket and bowed. He then went to the sacred rock and fell onto his knees before the stone tablet in reverent awe. After several minutes of silent prayer, he rose and left the room. One by one the dwarves behind him paid their respects to Behlin and fell to their knees before the sacred rock. Throughout the day and night, the dwarves filed past the casket and the sacred rock, singing as they went. When the last had passed, they buried Behlin.

The Dwarves Bid Behlin Farewell

Dehlin waited a respectful time after the King exited and then led Tom and the others to see him. After being admitted to an adjoining chamber Dehlin whispered, "Do as I do and say nothing unless the King addresses you."

The King stood in the center of the room surrounded by nobles and attendants to whom he was giving various commands. Dehlin and Tom stood at the entrance for several minutes until King Raegenheri noticed them and said in a loud voice, "Hail, Dehlin and friends! Advance and speak!"

Dehlin bowed and walked up to the King where he knelt on one knee and then rose. He waited for the others to follow his example and then said, "Great King! We rejoice at your return!"

Dehlin paused and was deeply moved. After taking a moment to gather himself he said, "I am honored and truly grateful for your appearance at my father's funeral."

King Raegenheri replied, "Your father was among the greatest of the prophets and teachers of our people. I am blessed to have seen the joy on his face that bears witness to his passage to the Creator. However, I must confess that I did not know of his passing until hearing your funeral song."

The King noticed Dehlin's confusion and said, "At the time of our departure from this place, Behlin foretold that the sacred rock would signal the time of our return from the deep places in the mountains. When we felt the earth shake, we knew it was time to return. The translation of part of the stone tablet also confirms this."

Noticing the seeing stone carried by Tom, he approached him and said, "I see that this human child wears a seeing stone. This also is a sign since our prophecies tell us that the first of the sons of light will appear in this place. All these things lead me to believe that it is time for us to fulfill our destiny in the Creator's service."

The King took Tom by the arm and walked over to a gilded chest. He took a key from a chain around his neck and unlocked it.

"Please open it."

Tom slowly opened the chest and saw a seeing stone identical to his on a golden chain.

The King removed it and said, "This is one of the twelve stones destined for the sons of light. It was entrusted to King Berin the Great by Prince Filane. Prince Filane was lord of the elves and lived with the dwarves after the Creator removed the humans from this world. When it was time for the elves to depart, he gave this to King Berin, who was my great, great grandfather, with instructions to never show it to anyone until a human child wearing an identical one should appear."

King Raegenheri held it up to a nearby torch mounted in the wall and continued, "When this was given to me by my father, he showed me that there is something written deep within this stone. It appears to be of the same unknown language as is on the tablet of the sacred rock. There is a prophecy that the first of the sons of light will be able to translate the writing."

Turning to Tom, the King gave him the stone and asked, "Can you read the inscription?"

Tom looked at the stone and then at Willet and shrugged his shoulders, "I have not noticed anything written within my stone nor do I see anything within this one."

The King replied, "The writing is not evident unless the stone is held near fire. Please hold it before your eyes and approach the flame."

Tom did as the King instructed and moved near the torch. He stood inches away from the flame with the stone before his eyes for several minutes before saying, "I still don't see anything."

The King replied, "Do not look through the stone. You must look deep within it for anything unusual and then focus on it."

Tom did as the King instructed. He stared into rather than through it for several more minutes. His eyes began to water and he was about to quit when he noticed a small cloudy spot appear. At first Tom thought his eyes were playing tricks on him, so he blinked to clear his vision but the spot just got larger and darker.

"I see something!" shouted Tom.

"What is it?" asked the King.

"I don't know," replied Tom.

The cloudy spot gradually resolved itself into some unknown inscription that resembled the writing on the stone tablet.

"I can see the writing but it is unknown to me! I wish I could read it."

Tom continued to stare intently into the stone. Slowly, the letters began to slowly move and change.

Tom exclaimed, "The writing is changing!"

"Can you read it?" asked Willet excitedly.

"What does it say?"

Tom turned and looked at them with amazement and said, "Wini! It says his name!"

Tom went over to Wini and held out the stone to him. Wini just looked at it and then turned to Willet with a pleading expression on his face.

"What should I do?" he asked Willet.

"Take the stone," Willet replied.

Wini reached out his hand and, as soon as he touched it, there was a bright burst of light that blinded them while the earth shook violently.

THE FOREST OF MORDULA

$\mathcal{M}$OLECH AND A HOST OF demons were in council in the Forest of Mordula near the Forbidden Mountains when a powerful earthquake interrupted them.

"Another earthquake comes from somewhere within the Forbidden Mountains, my lord," said Gorbash, who was one of Molech's lieutenants.

Molech hit him across the face and said, "Do you think I am stupid! I know the source of the quake. Tell me something I don't know!"

Gorbash quivered as he reported, "We have tried to enter the mountains from every direction, including from within the earth, but have not succeeded."

Molech seethed with rage anger and kicked around a score of demons to vent his rage before he said, "There is some presence or power that opposes us!"

Molech raised his voice and continued, "If we can not enter in spirit, then we shall send in the Titans!"

At this, a hundred demons flew off in all directions to gather creatures they controlled.

Gorbash approached meekly and said, "As you know, I have attended to the dwarf Miran faithfully for many years and have been instrumental in his conversion to *The Once and Forever Ruler.*"

Molech replied, "Yes, again you begin to annoy me with the obvious. You have been made a lieutenant in recognition of that accomplishment. Do not further waste my time with the past. Tell me something of value or I will beat you for your insolence!"

Gorbash cowered before Molech, which he knew pleased him, and said, "O great lord, send for the gnomes! They may prove to be more valuable than the Titans since they once lived in these mountains."

Molech considered this and said, "I believe you may have a good idea but I shall make it better! We know that the dwarves have changed and hidden their entrances so it will be difficult for even the gnomes. However, through deception perhaps the dwarves will reveal what we may fail to discover."

"What is your command?" asked Gorbash.

"I want you to place a strong desire in Miran to return in honor to the Forbidden Mountains before he dies. Stir up his humiliation at his embarrassing banishment. Tempt him with thoughts of revenge and of conquering the dwarves so they may be banished!

Then guide him to use deception to gain the trust of the dwarves by telling them that he has had a change of heart and now realizes he made a grievous error in promoting *The Once and Forever Ruler.* Once he has their trust, he can spy on them and then we can devise a plan of attack."

"Excellent plan my lord!" replied Gorbash.

"As always, your ideas are best. However, this plan will take considerable time to accomplish. Shall the Titans be recalled?"

"No! This is why you are limited to being a lieutenant Gorbash. You do not see new opportunities to improvise more devious strategies as I do!"

Molech continued, "We will use the Titans to devise a way to gain entrance by exploiting the compassion of the dwarves!"

THE SONS OF LIGHT

"MIN! IT SAYS MIN!" SHOUTED Tom as he held the stone that Min gave him up to the torch.

Min looked around with a sheepish grin and asked, "What does it mean?"

Willet replied, "It means the stone is destined for you."

"How can that be!" exclaimed Cearl in disbelief.

"The prophecies do not speak of a troll among the sons of light."

"Nor do they exclude such a possibility," replied Willet.

Willet looked warmly at Cearl and continued, "I, like you, have been taught that the elves will keep the seeing stones until the sons of light are revealed. Tradition teaches that humans are the sons of light. This has been an interpretation that has now been shown to be incorrect. The will of the Creator has been clearly revealed through the name inscribed in each stone."

"Remember the words of the stone tablet," said King Raegenheri.

He closed his eyes as if to visualize the words. His face beamed with joy as he spoke the translated words on the stone tablet with power and authority:

I will destroy the wisdom of the wise
The intelligence of the intelligent I
will frustrate,
For my ways are not your ways
Nor are my thoughts your thoughts.
Great and marvelous are my plans,
For as high as the heavens are
above the earth
So are my thoughts beyond your
understanding.

As the king recited these words, everyone else in the room fell on their knees and were deeply moved. Many wept in awe at the wonder and majestic power of these words. The three seeing stones emitted a brilliant, green light that was too intense to behold. Once again, the sacred rock shook the earth until the last of the words were spoken.

After several moments of reverent silence following the recital of the sacred words, the King opened his eyes and said, "Let none doubt the Creator's will in this matter. Behold! The first of the sons of light have been revealed!"

The King continued, "Arise Tom, Wini and Min!"

"Amen! So be it!" shouted everyone in the room. They began cheering as the King motioned for them to stand beside him.

The King proclaimed, "From this day until death take us

or new life save us, let all swear to bring about the new age heralded by these sons of light!"

"Amen! We swear with all that we have and all that we are!"

AERIAL ADVENTURE

$\mathcal{D}$EHLIN LED TOM AND CEARL through Hadrian's Keep. It had been several months since Behlin's funeral but they still could not figure out the maze of rooms and hallways within the Keep. Tom was amazed at how quickly the dwarves had occupied and cleaned up the Keep. He would never have believed that it was an ancient tomb just a few months ago.

"Dwarves are certainly an enterprising race," he thought to himself as they climbed to the upper levels of the Keep.

"They are always busy, yet warm and friendly. They like to sit and talk, especially over a tankard of ale, or gladly stop what they are doing to help someone in need. They enjoy being busy but enjoy helping each other even more!"

Tom thought about how different this was from the Village of Downs End where everyone was too busy to help others unless there was an emergency. As he thought of home, he experienced a bout of homesickness. Although he desired to see his parents, he trusted Willet who said it was too dangerous to attempt to see them before his training was complete.

"Best to put thoughts of home aside for now and focus on your studies," Willet would always say.

As they continued to ascend the Keep, Tom reflected on how fast the days had passed since Behlin's death. He had settled into a daily routine of studies of various sorts led by Willet and several dwarf scribes. There was also skill training in crafts and military tactics led by Dehlin and other warriors. However, it was the opportunities to explore during the weekly excursions around the Keep that Tom enjoyed the most.

Today was such a day. Tom had never been so high in the Keep and frequently stopped to look out the windows. As he looked down, he could see numerous gardens containing evergreen trees, fountains, and flowers of many colors. From this vantage point, he could see many dwarves busy in their gardens or basking in the sunshine and solitude of these patches of greenery perched among the rocks.

There were also many rock spires of various shapes and heights. At the top of some of the spires there were unique triangular pendants with the symbols and colors of various dwarf clans. Tom marveled at the number of different gardens. He had also never seen so many dwarves before and noted that they were not visible except from above.

"Master Tom, you must not dawdle or we shall be late," scolded Dehlin.

"Late for what?" asked Tom.

"You will see. Hurry along!" replied Dehlin.

After a few more turns, ascents, and descents, Dehlin suddenly disappeared although Tom was but a few steps behind him. Tom soon discovered that the hallway made a sharp bend to the right and then to the left. After traversing this zigzag, he found himself standing in a beautiful garden surrounded by sharp rock pinnacles that formed a wall around it several hundred feet high!

Tom had never seen such a beautiful and tranquil place. There were water fountains and pools surrounded by various fruit trees and a profusion of flowers of every color and shape imaginable.

"Welcome, Master Tom and Cearl!" said King Raegenheri.

In a clearing just ahead stood Willet, Wini, Min, and Penda along with several dwarf guides.

Tom asked, "Where are we?"

"In one of several hidden plateaus at the top of the Keep," replied Dehlin.

"It is in places like this that we grow some of our crops."

The King pointed to the sky and said, "What do you see?"

Tom replied, "Nothing but blue sky."

"Keep looking!" commanded the King as he put his fingers to his lips and gave a shrill whistle.

At first, Tom saw nothing, but then a black speck appeared against the clear blue sky. The black speck grew rapidly in size and separated into a group of birds. The birds grew progressively larger as they descended with great speed. Tom soon became a bit unnerved when he saw that these birds were the largest eagles he had ever seen!

As they landed, the King bowed and said, "Hail brothers! You honor us!"

In reply, the eagles spread their wings and lowered their heads. Tom was struck by the majestic presence of these birds, which stood six feet tall and had wing spans approaching twenty feet!

The King turned to Dehlin and said, "Please demonstrate the proper way to ride."

Dehlin walked up to the nearest eagle and, after exchanging bows, he jumped onto his back. He produced a short rope from his pocket, which he looped around the neck of the eagle.

One by one, they followed Dehlin's example with assistance from the dwarves who handed them each a short rope. The last one was Min, who looked embarrassed as he approached one of the eagles.

"I'm afraid I am too large for you," he said sheepishly.

The King replied, "We have made special arrangements for you."

Another eagle moved beside the one next to Min. He held a sling in his beak. Each eagle took one end of the sling in their mouth. Min gingerly sat in the sling between them with a look of fear on his face.

"I don't think this will work. I'm too heavy!" he said as he looked at the King.

"Nonsense! You underestimate the power of your companions," replied the King. "A single eagle can lift a cow or bull in a sling such as yours thousands of feet and move it up to a hundred miles between isolated mountain meadows. These two eagles have agreed to carry you this way so you can sit comfortably. However, if you prefer, one of them will carry you like a beast in a belly sling."

"No, thank you! This will do quite nicely!" replied Min, who was horrified by the thought of being suspended on his belly beneath just one eagle.

The King said, "Very well! Follow me!"

THE FORBIDDEN MOUNTAINS

*T*OM WAS AMAZED AT HOW quickly and easily they ascended above the surrounding peaks. At first, he was afraid and concentrated on holding onto the ends of the rope around the eagle's neck. After they had leveled off and he saw the spectacular beauty of the mountains and valleys, he relaxed and was captivated by the scenery.

"Wondrous, isn't it!"

Tom looked around but could not tell where the voice came from. The others were above and below him but they were tens of yards away. The voice seemed quite near and was not affected by the wind rushing by his ears.

"My name is Skreel. I am honored to accompany you!" said the voice.

Tom continued to look around but could not see anyone who could be speaking to him.

"Where are you?" Tom asked.

"You are sitting on me," replied Skreel.

Tom realized that the voice was inside his head and that the eagle was communicating with him telepathically.

Skreel continued, "My ancestors fought with the elves in the battle of the Forest of Mordula in order to preserve mankind from Devlin's forces. After this battle, they retreated with the elves into these mountains, which have since been our domain."

Tom asked, "Do you serve the dwarves?"

Skreel let out a screech as if to emphasize his response.

"No! We call none but the Creator our Master! The dwarves and all kindred creatures that follow the teachings of *The Past and Future King* are our brothers. We hold all such creatures to be equal and treat them with honor and respect. We keep watch over the passes and secret places to prevent any foul creatures from entering our land."

"Where are we going?" asked Tom.

"Deep into the mountains," replied Skreel. "You will see many secret places visible only from the air."

The mountains ahead were snow capped and, as they approached them, became progressively higher and more rugged. They flew over several valleys that were covered with snow so deep that no trees were visible. However, there was one valley just ahead that was completely covered with a blanket of low clouds. They made straight for this valley and soon were descending through a thick layer of mist.

Tom was surprised by how warm and humid the air felt as they descended through the mist. Suddenly they broke through the clouds. Several hundred feet below them was a lush green valley covered with mushrooms. There were mushrooms of every shape, size, and color. Some grew like trees and shrubs while others covered the ground.

They landed beside a bubbling pool that emitted steam into the air.

Skreel said, "This valley has numerous hot springs and vents that humidify the air and make it ideal for growing mushrooms!"

Tom could see some dwarves emerge from a hidden door in the rocks. They began to pick the mushrooms and put them into carts.

Skreel continued, "The dwarves harvest the mushrooms daily and carry them to markets deep inside the mountains."

After a while, the dwarves pushed a cart full of mushrooms towards a rock wall and suddenly disappeared back into the mountain.

Tom asked, "How do they do that?"

Skreel replied, "Dwarves have little knowledge or use for magic except when it involves these mountains. At this sort of magic they excel."

"Hold on!" shouted Skreel as he and the others suddenly took off.

After flying around the valley, they suddenly soared upward through the cloud layer and resumed their flight over the mountains.

Skreel said, "There are many such hidden valleys within these mountains that can not be reached except by air or from tunnels. In some valleys crops or livestock are grown, while others are completely untouched."

"Where are we going now?" asked Tom.

Skreel replied, "To the far side of the mountains near the Forest of Mordula."

After flying for several hours, the mountains gradually declined in height. The snow in the valleys diminished and then disappeared. The valleys on this side contained lush green meadows, alpine lakes, and fir forests.

"Look directly below in the pass between the mountains! What do you see?" asked Skreel.

Tom saw some dark shapes on the ground below but they were too high to tell what they were.

"Hang on! We'll dive to investigate!" shouted Skreel.

Tom was surprised to see that the shapes were several dozen dead werewolves. They appeared to have been ambushed.

As they gathered in a group near one of them, the King dismounted and said, "Werewolves, orcs, trolls, and gnomes have recently begun to invade our lands. They come with growing frequency and increasing numbers. We have learned that they are searching for a way into the mountains so they can spy on us. However, thanks to the eagles we have been able to ambush and destroy them."

Willet said, "This werewolf has been shot by a gnome arrow and there is a gnome ax lying on the ground beside that one."

"Quite so!" replied the King. "We have made it look like the gnomes did this. We do likewise with orc arrows and weapons when we ambush the gnomes. It makes our task easier since it keeps them fighting each other instead of us."

The king remounted his eagle and said, "The day grows old and we have yet one more visit to make."

Skreel carries Tom on an aerial adventure

DINWALD'S DEEP

"To Dinwald's Deep and double quick!" shouted the King.

They shot up into the sky with such speed that it made Tom's eyes water. The sun was just touching the tops of the tallest mountain peaks when they suddenly dove towards a black hole below. As they approached it, Tom saw that it was a vertical shaft about one hundred feet across. A small mountain stream dropped into it on one side. As they entered the shaft, Tom could feel the damp, humid air and hear the spraying cascade of water as it hit rocks and ledges on its way down the shaft. Tom became alarmed by the speed at which they were descending blindly into the blackness.

"Where is the bottom?" asked Tom.

"Do not fear! The light from the annwn will soon appear," replied Skreel.

Tom saw a faint glow in the distance that grew rapidly in brightness. When they reached the source of the light, Tom saw that the walls of the shaft sparkled with thousands of glowing rocks. Also, the air became warmer and less humid despite the spray from the cascading waterfall.

"The annwn are rocks found deep inside these mountains. They provide heat and light that enables the dwarves to live and even grow plants totally underground if they wish."

Skreel opened his wings and began to slow their descent. When they reached the bottom, Tom was astonished to see a stone, arched bridge across a crystal-clear pool fed by the waterfall.

On the opposite side of the bridge was a massive, arched doorway that led into the mountain. Two ranks of dwarves in full battle dress stood at attention on either side of the doorway from the bridge to the entrance.

Tom said, "Apparently, our arrival has been expected."

"One of my kin flew directly here to announce our visit when we departed from Hadrian's Keep," replied Skreel.

They landed on the far side of the bridge and, once Tom dismounted, Skreel bowed and said, "This is where we part. Think of me if you have need and I shall come."

Tom returned the bow and said, "Farewell, Skreel. I have been blessed by our encounter. I shall think of you fondly and call you friend."

Once the rest of the party dismounted, the King faced the eagles, raised both of his arms, and said, "You have honored us with your service. Please accept my deepest gratitude and my blessing."

The eagles bowed in unison and spread their wings as when they met. They gave a deafening scream and flew quickly out of sight.

The King turned to Tom and the others and said,

"Welcome to Dinwald's Deep! This place is among the oldest and most esteemed of our strongholds."

He led them between the two ranks of dwarves through the doorway and into a vast hall with rows of columns hundreds of feet high. Everywhere the walls and ceiling were studded with annwn. Tom noted that the light cast by these rocks was far better than lamps or torches.

Within the great hall were thousands of dwarves lined up behind two ranks of warriors that formed a path through the crowd. As the King entered the hall the dwarves knelt on one knee and uncovered their heads as a sign of respect. They passed through the great hall and into a narrow passage that got progressively smaller until Min and Willet had to bend over to pass through.

The tunnel ended abruptly in a small room. The King turned and waited for the others to gather. He then proceeded to touch several annwn in the walls and ceiling. After touching the third one, a stone slab in the floor near their feet slowly opened.

The King said, "Lord Dinwald was the commander of the elf army that fought Devlin's forces in the Forest of Mordula. We are about to enter his final resting place and that of many of his kin who fell in that great battle."

As Tom descended a ladder mounted into the rock below the entrance, he felt as though he was entering a sleeping chamber rather than a tomb. He sensed that this was a place of rest for those who had faithfully carried out the roles their Creator had given them. There was no sadness but rather a sense of expectation that someday they would rise to a new and better life.

There were thousands of tombs spread across an expansive

cavern that looked even larger than the great hall they had just passed through. Each tomb was a rectangular stone crypt upon which some elfish words were inscribed. The armor and weapons of each elf were carefully laid on the lid of each crypt.

As Tom looked around, he noticed that the stone around his neck felt heavy. When he pulled it out of his shirt, it was glowing.

"My stone also glows!" whispered Min.

"Mine too!" replied Wini.

Tom looked at Min's stone and saw that its glow was focused into a beam of light that reached out into the distance.

"Look!" said Wini. "The glow from our stones is narrowing into beams of light!"

"I wonder what it means," said Min.

Willet said, "I suggest we follow the light beams and find out. Min's appears to be closest so let's follow his first."

As they followed the light beam from Min's stone the King explained, "Every tomb is inscribed with a tribute to each elf. The armor and weapons placed on the lid of each crypt indicate rank and personal information. For example, the helmet of each elf is typically inscribed with their name or some personal trait or characteristic."

Wini interrupted his dialogue and said, "Look! The light from Min's stone falls on this tomb!"

They paused and observed a moment of silence as they stared at the crypt illuminated by Min's stone. Min cautiously and reverently approached the head of the crypt and ran his hand over the inscription.

"What does it say?" he asked.

Willet translated,

Here I rest,
A faithful friend
I did my best,
To serve and bless...

Min interrupted and shouted, "My name! This helmet says my name!"

They gathered around Min and saw that part of the forehead of the helmet was dented. It looked like it had taken a glancing blow from a heavy object or weapon that had deformed part of it.

The letters *MIN* were inscribed on the helmet but the blow had obliterated the rest of the letters. When Min touched the helmet, it began to glow with the same green light that came from Min's stone.

"It seems the armor responds favorably to your touch," observed the King. "Perhaps you should try it on."

Min picked up the helmet and thought it was superb despite its imperfection. A look of sadness came across his face and he said, "I'm afraid it's too small."

The King replied, "If it is meant for you it will fit."

Min shrugged his shoulders and then slowly lowered the helmet onto his head.

"It fits!" he beamed.

"Try on the rest of the armor," urged the King.

Min held the breastplate to his chest. The size and shape were obviously made for an elf and not a troll.

"There is no way this can fit me!" said Min.

"Nevertheless, try it on!" commanded the King.

When Min placed it up against his chest, it seemed to expand to fit his frame.

"This is unbelievable!" shouted Min. He excitedly put on the rest of the armor and stood before them beaming from ear to ear. He looked quite formidable but also somewhat odd due to the strange combination of elfish armor that had somewhat altered his troll shape.

"I wish Lord Swefred could see this!" Cearl exclaimed.

"Yes, I dare say that the look on his face would set me laughing for a week!" replied Willet.

After they had a good laugh, the King seemed to catch himself and resumed his royal manner and said, "Ahem! Enough frivolities! Let's see where Tom's stone leads us."

As they continued, Tom wondered where the light from his stone was leading them. He was astonished at the seemingly endless rows of crypts.

"There must be thousands of elves buried in this place," he told himself.

At the center of the cavern, there was a raised platform on which a very ornate crypt rested. It was embossed with gold and silver characters and symbols. Tom was about to walk by when he noticed that the King, Willet, Cearl, and Penda stopped to pay homage.

"This is the resting place of Lord Dinwald," said King Raegenheri.

Tom and the rest of the group joined them and stood silently for a few moments.

Cearl then read the inscription:

Here lies Lord Dinwald most kind and noble.
He counted not the value of his life to save those less blessed.
May he rest in peace until the end and beginning of all things.

One by one they knelt and kissed the crypt, and then resumed their quest. They followed the beam of light until it rested on a wall at the far end of the cavern.

Tom turned and said, "Looks like we are at a dead end."

"Appearances are not always what they seem," replied the King.

He placed his hand on the spot indicated by the light beam and the rock slowly began to move, revealing a small door.

"After you, Master Tom," said the King.

Tom passed through a short tunnel and entered a small room. In its center was a tomb on a raised platform similar to that of Lord Dinwald, but less ornate. The light from Tom's stone rested on the tomb.

After they were all in the room, the King said, "Approach the tomb, Master Tom."

As Tom stepped on the first step leading to the top of the platform a brilliant light burst from the tomb. It was so intense that it temporarily blinded all of them except for Tom. The light from Tom's stone also increased in brilliance to match the light from the crypt.

Tom noticed that the light from his stone blended with that from the crypt so that it did not blind him. While the others were still blinded and dazed, Tom continued to approach the crypt. He had a strange sensation that he was lying inside of it.

After ascending the steps, he saw that the top of the crypt was slightly taller than him. He stood on his tiptoes and peered across the top. Before him was the most elegant suit of armor he had ever seen. On the breastplate rested the source of the light.

"Another seeing stone!" he whispered to himself in amazement.

Tom removed the stone by picking it up by its chain. As he held it before his eyes, it started to move towards him as if attracted by some magnetic force. The stone on his chest also started to move towards the one in his hand. Before Tom could react, the two stones came together and fused into a spherical stone twice the size of both elliptical stones. However, the chain and leather necklaces remained attached. Tom placed both necklaces around his neck and felt a surge of energy fill his body, giving him an elated sense of peace and joy.

Reaching over the top of the tomb, he grabbed the helmet and held it in his hands. It was made of gold with silver elfish words inscribed in a band that ran around the entire helmet. It also had a plume of multicolored ribbons attached to the top. Each ribbon was embroidered with silver elfish letters. Above and below the band of letters on the helmet were various figures of elves, eagles, men, and other creatures that depicted battles and feats of bravery. He noticed that he had picked up the helmet such that he was looking at the back of it so he slowly turned it around. As he looked at the front, he froze and stood transfixed, holding it before his eyes.

Willet recovered his sight first and noticed Tom standing like a statue in awe and wonder. He walked over to Tom and looked at the helmet.

Willet smiled as he read the word inscribed on its brow.

"Egric," he said.

EPILOGUE

OVER THE NEXT TEN YEARS they remained at Hadrian's Keep. Tom grew in stature, knowledge, and power as he learned the ways of men, elves, and dwarves. Although elves age much slower than men, the appearance of Cearl and Penda seemed to match the growth of Tom.

There was some unknown power at work among them that helped them to understand and accept each other's differences. Their friendship and dedication to each other grew until they thought of themselves as blood relatives.

Min found the friendship that he longed for and he continued to work hard to please the others. Wini looked after Tom and Min like a big brother. Cearl and Penda dedicated themselves to training the others in elfish skills, such as telepathy and astral projection.

Willet became like a father to them. He took great pride and pleasure in their development. Willet's zeal to share the vast knowledge he had accumulated was challenging and intriguing to all of them.

Occasionally, Wini would worry about his sheep, Tom would miss his parents, or Cearl and Penda would ask about returning to their kinfolk. Only Min seemed perfectly content to be with his first and only friends. Willet continued to insist that they remain within the Forbidden Mountains. Although they each had different reasons for wishing to contact friends and relatives, they trusted and respected Willet's wishes.

Amhas tried to sell his information regarding the seeing stones, but whenever he mentioned Hadrian's Keep, nobody believed him. He soon became frustrated and turned to other pursuits.

Crodha took the Witch of Ogherune to the place of his death. The Witch conjured the image of Min with the seeing stone but they did not know his name. They followed his path to the cave in the pass where it ended on the cave floor. Crodha and the Witch reported their findings to Molech who ordered a search for any word of a troll with a seeing stone, but nothing more was discovered.

Likewise, Lord Ceowulf and his supporters diligently searched for Tom and the others but to no avail.

The ensuing decade was a time of relative peace in the first age of the Earth. There were few skirmishes and fewer earthquakes and other natural disasters. The attention of Molech was focused on the world of men in the second age of the Earth.

The Brotherhood of Andhun launched their long planned movement to unite all the kingdoms of the second age of the Earth. They had spent many years scheming to place their members in strategic positions of political and philosophical power.

They initiated a coordinated plan to convert all of

mankind to the beliefs found in *The Once and Forever Ruler*. As their plans unfolded, those who opposed them were disgraced, assassinated, or persecuted. The resulting chaos ended the thousand years of peace enjoyed by mankind. A new era of ideological intolerance and warfare became the fate of mankind. These conditions set the stage for the appearance of the sons of light.

BOOK REVIEW REQUEST

THANK YOU FOR TAKING YOUR valuable time to read my book. I hope you enjoyed reading it as much as I enjoyed writing it. What did you think? I want to know. I would appreciate if you would take a few minutes to write a review for this book on Amazon.com. Thank you in advance for taking the time to respond. I look forward to reading your review.

CHARACTERS

Abban—King who invades the kingdom of Redwald to force it to submit to the Brotherhood of Andhun.

Aigneis—Angels who remained obedient to God. The elves and fairies are the physical descendants of these good angels on earth.

Alric—King of Strathyre and Oriana's uncle who is one of three kings opposed to the Brotherhood of Andhun.

Amhas—Renegade troll who leads a group of bandit trolls.

Andhun—Wizard formerly of the Order Of Alastrine and once had the seeing stone carried by Tom. Founder and head of the brotherhood based on *The Once And Forever Ruler*.

Behlin—Dwarf scribe who became Willet's friend and leader of those who study the sacred runes of Hadrian's Keep.

Berin—Ancient king of the dwarves and ancestor of King Raegenheri.

Bill Barley—Peddler who delivered books to Willet in Downs End.

Boroc—Pyrigian who leads a band of orcs in search of Min.

Bournemouth—Trusted advisor of King Alric of Strathyre who secretly was a member of the Botherhood of Andhun.

Bruddai—King who invades the kingdom of Redwald to force it to submit to the Brotherhood of Andhun.

Caelin—Elf prince and ruler of the Valley of Glainne.

Cearl—Elf and son of Prince Caelin assigned to protect Tom.

Cebu—Grandson of Miran who is taken into the Forbidden Mountains upon the death of his grandfather. He seeks to betray the dwarves by revealing an entrance to the Forbidden Mountains.

Ceowulf—Elf of high rank and reputation who strictly follows the traditions and beliefs of his people.

Crodha—Orc general who led the attack on the darach trees and obtained Lord Swefred's seeing stone.

Cragmar—Troll searching for an entrance to the Forbidden Mountains.

Cyric—Leader of Camlin which is a village of thieves and bandits. He is the illegitimate son of King Vulpes.

Dehlin—Dwarf son of Behlin and leader of those who guard Hadrian's Keep.

Demonians—Evil angels who followed Devlin in rebellion against their Creator.

Devlin—Demon leader who desires to rule the earth and author of *The Once And Forever Ruler.*

Dinwald—Elf lord who commanded the forces opposed to Devlin in the Battle of Mordula Forest.

Edric—Elf who follows Lord Ceowulf to the Forbidden Mountains and secretly watches the events surrounding the death of Miran.

Egric—Elf lord who died fighting against Devlin's forces at the Battle of Mordula Forest.

Eni—Elf companion of Cearl who helps Tom escape from werewolves.

Etain—Fairy who serves as scout and messenger for the elves.

Filane—Elf lord who lived with the dwarves in the Forbidden Mountains following the battle of the forest of Modula.

Garash—Head of a band of orc pirates who follow Miran to

Hadrian's Keep searching for an entrance to the Forbidden Mountains.

Gorbash—Demon of Pyrrigian rank charged with guarding Throm and was influential in the conversion of the dwarf Miran to the ways of *The Once And Forever Ruler*.

Hadrian—Dwarf king who built a hidden fortress in the side of Forbidden Mountains named Hadrian's Keep.

Haggert—Demon possessed elder of the Village of Camlin.

Hockley—Constable of the Village of Kilkenny.

Hostyn—King assassinated in his palace in Lochlemond by traitors loyal to Andhun.

Ian—Lieutenant of Cyric of Camlin assigned to lead Oriana and Tom to Lochlemond.

Izora—Captain of the men-at-arms in the service of King Alric of Strathyre.

Kerwin—Blind man found by Tom on the road to Strathyre.

Kork—Drunken troll at the Black Horse Inn.

Lagopus—Gnome who idolizes Andhun and serves him as his personal attendant.

Linette—Elf princess who raised Willet and rules Taliesin

Olaf—name given to Oriana by Willet as part of her disguise as a boy.

Min—Troll who longs to find friendship.

Miran—Leader and founder of the gnomes. He was once was a dwarf scribe that converted to *The Once And Forever Ruler* which resulted in his banishment from the Forbidden Mountains.

Molech—Chief demon second in command to Devlin and he is in charge of evil spirits roaming the earths.

Nabloth—Young female troll whose mother is Sharat.

Og—Elder female troll from village lead by Sharat.

Olric—Son of King Thymallis and a member of the Brotherhood of Andhun.

Oriana—Princess of Eisendrath and daughter of King Thymallis.

Osric—Elf companion of Cearl who helps Tom escape from werewolves.

Peig—Elder female troll from the village lead by Sharat.

Penda—Elf assigned to protect Wini.

Pyrigians—elite demons known for their cruelty.

Raegenheri—King of the dwarves.

Ragbar—Demon of Pyrigian rank who was assigned to watch over Andhun.

Ronan—One of the seven kings who support the Brotherhood of Andhun. Led his army against King Alric.

Sharat—Female troll shamman and mother of Nabloth.

Shylah—Troll converted to the ways of The Past & Future King by Min.

Skreel—Eagle and friend of Tom.

Swefred—Elf lord renown as a warrior and keeper of a seeing stone.

Throm—Father of Tom and farmer in the Village of Downs End.

Thymallis—King of Eisendrath and father of Oriana and Olric.

Titans—Creatures such as orcs, vampires & trolls formed by the union of evil angels who took human form and intermarried with mankind.

Tom—Son of Throm the farmer and bearer of a seeing stone.

Tondbert—Dwarf who was transformed into a tree by magic.

Torin—King of Redwald who opposes the Brotherhood of Andhun.

Trossacks—Friend of Ian who is the leader of a band of wandering musicians.

Ultan—Troll leader who lead a band of trolls in search of an entrance to the Forbidden Mountains.

Vulpes—King of Meglondon and leader of the kings who support Andhun. Father of Cyric and suitor of Oriana.

Whon—One of the seven kings who support the Brotherhood of Andhun. Led his army against King Alric.

Willet—Scribe of the Village of Downs End, wizard of the Order of Alastrine and mentor to Tom.

Wini—Shepherd of Redwald and companion of Tom.

Witch Of Ogherune—Spirit of a powerful witch who can conjure images of past events.

ACKNOWLEDGEMENTS

*T*HIS STORY, LIKE LIFE, IS a journey of discovery that has been revealed one step at a time. The Bible and the Holy Spirit in my life have provided the foundation for the development of this story. The unfolding of this story has given me great pleasure due to a divine interaction that has provided the energy and inspiration behind this book.

My active imagination, coupled with a fascination for fantasy and science fiction, have been formative in my interest of this type of book. It was my son, Jacob Mueller, who was instrumental in encouraging me to actually attempt to write a fantasy book. We both decided to begin writing such books together. It was this bonding that awakened a desire to take Biblical themes and weave them into a tale that merges human dreams with fantasy. In many ways, my experiences have convinced me that there is much more to human life than meets the eye.

ABOUT THE AUTHOR

*T*HE ORIGINS OF MY INTEREST in fiction are rooted in my early childhood. As a child, I loved to sleep over at my friend's house on Friday nights and watch the late night science fiction movies. I have fond memories of ducking in and out of my sleeping bag on the living room floor while being both captivated and frightened.

In college, I discovered C.S. Lewis and soon was experiencing other worlds in his Space Trilogy and *Chronicles of Narnia*. These were my favorite multi-book stories until a friend suggested I try reading *The Hobbit* by J.R.R. Tolkien. This led to *The Lord of the Rings* trilogy which I read several times prior to the movies. Hobbits, elves, orcs, trolls were like the races and cultures of man in that they were related but different. Interwoven throughout these stories were the struggle of good and evil as well as the discovery of purpose and realizing one's potential.

My education and career over the past forty years have been in the Environmental Sciences which are hardly conducive to fiction writing. I graduated with two MS degrees from the University of Wisconsin and worked as a consultant and then as an environmental specialist for a mid-western utility company. After raising two children, I found myself a grandparent with a successful wife who spent several days a week traveling as a director for a dental corporation. My wife claims that being a grandpa has awakened the right side of my brain and has helped me discover my second childhood. I find there is some truth to this as I can act goofy, spoil my grandchildren and then give them back to their parents.

While driving alone on a work trip, a thought occurred to me that I should write a book about what the Bible says about various subjects. I have read the Bible daily for over thirty years, spoken in many churches as a member of the Gideons, taught Sunday School and served as a deacon, so I felt I could help others to understand what I consider the most important book ever written. Two years later my first book, *Truth Seeker: Bible Topics*, was written.

For me writing is a passion. Over the past thirteen years, I have written eight books and over twenty articles for the New York Times about Christianity and Christian Pulse web sites. The *Dawn Herald Triology* is a Lord of the Rings style tale that weaves Christian themes into a multi-book series on the inter-play between reality and fantasy worlds. The spiritual realm, like fantasy, is not real to some but intrigues many people because there is a deep innate sense in mankind that there is a greater reality.

Fictional writing is based on developing interesting characters and then visualizing how they progress in their roles. In other words, the characters carry the plot and writing is like watching scenes in a play unfold. My non-fictional writing revolves around the Bible which I have studied daily for over thirty years. I love to learn and share the awesome truths of the Bible. I am amazed and humbled by what I have written as I see myself as a scribe recording what God has given for our edification.

My *Truth Seeker Series* consists of five non-fictional books based on the Bible. *Truth Seeker: Bible Topics* summarizes what the Bible says about a wide range of topics with lots of Bible references. *Truth Seeker: Mormon Scriptures & The Bible* summarizes the books upon which Mormonism is based and compares them to the Bible. *Truth Seeker: New Testament Apocrypha* summarizes selected books from the early centuries of Christianity and seeks objective reasons why these books were not included in the Bible. *Truth Seeker: Objections To Christianity* and *Truth Seeker: More Objections To Christianity* are a dialogue with my father who was a critic of Christianity. He summarized his beliefs and problems with the Bible and left me with a written legacy. Thus, these books complete decades of debates that we had prior to his death.

Printed in the United States
By Bookmasters